Y0-BRG-027

"You need to leave. Now."

"I can't just leave you..." he said.

"Why not?" she asked. "You didn't come here to protect me. You came here to force me to provide you with an alibi. I can't do that. I can't perjure myself and swear you never left me that night."

"I didn't want you to perjure yourself," he said. "I wanted you to tell the truth."

"I have," she said.

He wished he could be certain that he believed her.

"So why are you still here?" she asked.

He gestured toward her bedroom, to where their daughter lay sleeping. He couldn't put into words what he already felt for his daughter—the protectiveness, the affection, the devotion....

"Until a few hours ago you didn't even know she existed," she reminded him.

"Whose fault was that?" he asked, the question slipping out with his bitterness.

LISA CHILDS

BABY BREAKOUT

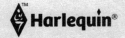

TORONTO NEW YORK LONDON
AMSTERDAM PARIS SYDNEY HAMBURG
STOCKHOLM ATHENS TOKYO MILAN MADRID
PRAGUE WARSAW BUDAPEST AUCKLAND

If you purchased this book without a cover you should be aware
that this book is stolen property. It was reported as "unsold and
destroyed" to the publisher, and neither the author nor the
publisher has received any payment for this "stripped book."

To my babies, who are now amazing young women.
Ashley and Chloe, I am so proud and blessed to be your
mother. There is nothing the two of you can't accomplish
with your intelligence and determination.

ISBN-13: 978-0-373-69611-6

Recycling programs
for this product may
not exist in your area.

BABY BREAKOUT

Copyright © 2012 by Lisa Childs-Theeuwes

All rights reserved. Except for use in any review, the reproduction or
utilization of this work in whole or in part in any form by any electronic,
mechanical or other means, now known or hereafter invented, including
xerography, photocopying and recording, or in any information storage
or retrieval system, is forbidden without the written permission of the
publisher, Harlequin Enterprises Limited, 225 Duncan Mill Road,
Don Mills, Ontario, Canada M3B 3K9.

This is a work of fiction. Names, characters, places and incidents are
either the product of the author's imagination or are used fictitiously,
and any resemblance to actual persons, living or dead, business
establishments, events or locales is entirely coincidental.

This edition published by arrangement with Harlequin Books S.A.

For questions and comments about the quality of this book please contact
us at Customer_eCare@Harlequin.ca.

® and TM are trademarks of the publisher. Trademarks indicated with
® are registered in the United States Patent and Trademark Office, the
Canadian Trade Marks Office and in other countries.

www.Harlequin.com

Printed in U.S.A.

ABOUT THE A

Bestselling, award-winning author
paranormal and contemporary romance
Books. She lives on thirty acres in west M
her husband, two daughters, a talkative Siame
long-haired Chihuahua who thinks she's a rottw
Lisa loves hearing from readers, who can contact h
through her website, www.lisachilds.com, or snail mail
address, P.O. Box 139, Marne, MI 49435.

Books by Lisa Childs

HARLEQUIN INTRIGUE

*Outlaws

Don't miss any of our special offers. Write to us at the
following address for information on our newest releases.

Harlequin Reader Service
U.S.: 3010 Walden Ave., P.O. Box 1325, Buffalo, NY 14269
Canadian: P.O. Box 609, Fort Erie, Ont. L2A 5X3

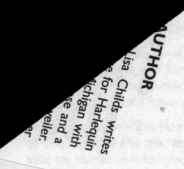

THE AUTHOR

Lisa Childs writes ... for Harlequin ... Michigan with ...se and a ...reiler.

... of murders ... hero escapes ... find the ... his name.

... doesn't remember enough ... murders ... provide Jed the ... she has proof they were tog...

Isobel Towsley—The toddler doesn't know who her father is, but Jed does the moment he first sees the child, who is the spitting image of his sister.

Macy Kleyn—She hasn't given up on proving her brother's innocence even though her fiancé is determined to put Jed back behind bars until that can be done.

Warden Jefferson James—The jailed former jailor puts out a hit on Jed so that the convict can't testify against him.

Marcus Leighton—Instead of representing him, Jed's lawyer might have helped frame him.

Brandon Henderson—The murder victim embezzled money from Jed's clients, and that money has never been found.

Prologue

The high-pitched beep of a breaking-news bulletin drew Erica Towsley's attention to the television screen. "During a prison riot tonight at Blackwoods Penitentiary in northern Michigan, cop killer Jedidiah Kleyn was among several prisoners to escape."

Jedidiah Kleyn.

Legs shaking, Erica dropped onto the edge of her sofa. She grabbed a pillow and clasped it against her chest as she struggled to breathe.

No. No. No. Not Jedidiah...

The report continued, "He is considered extremely dangerous."

Goose bumps lifted on her skin. *Dangerous* was an understatement for Jedidiah Kleyn's capacity for violence. Images flitted through her mind, as she recalled the graphic photographs she had been shown of the scene of the horrific crimes Jedidiah had been convicted of committing.

"If anyone believes they have seen this man or any of the other escaped..."

Ears buzzing with her pounding pulse, Erica could catch only snatches of what the serious-faced anchorwoman said.

"...contact authorities immediately. Do not approach these men..."

What if one of these men approached her? Would she have time to contact authorities before he killed her?

Chapter One

"Jed, let me bring you in," DEA agent Rowe Cusack's voice crackled in the beat-up pay-phone receiver.

Because everyone had cell phones nowadays, Jed had been lucky to find a pay phone, let alone one that was still working. But then this small mid-Michigan town was a throwback to about fifty years ago. With bright-colored awnings on its storefronts that faced out onto cobblestone streets, Miller's Valley might as well have been called Mayberry.

"You're not safe out there," Rowe continued.

Even at night, with the antique street lamps barely burning holes into the darkness, it was hard to imagine any danger here. Despite the cold and blowing snow, in any other city, people would have still been out—selling or buying things or services that shouldn't be commodities. Jedidiah Kleyn would like to believe that there was actually a place where no crime happened, where no evil existed, but he'd learned the hard way that nothing and nobody were ever as innocent as they might appear. And at times, some things and some people weren't as guilty, either.

"Is that because I'm a cop killer?" Jed asked quietly with a quick glance around him to make sure nobody overheard. But the cobblestone street was really deserted. No one lurked in the shadows here, as they had at Blackwoods.

This town, on the outskirts of Grand Rapids, Michigan, was so rural that everyone was early to bed, early to rise. So hopefully no one, inside their little houses behind their picket fences, was awake yet to notice the stranger in the borrowed dark wool jacket with the knit cap pulled low over his face, walking the snow-dusted streets of their town.

"You're not a killer." The certainty in the lawman's voice eased some of Jed's anxiety.

"That's not what a jury of my peers and a judge decided three years ago." He had been convicted of killing his business partner and a police officer who must have happened upon the murder.

"I've been going through the case file and the court transcripts," the agent said.

For the past three years he'd wanted to get his hands on those files, but his lawyer hadn't been able to get the records past the guards at Blackwoods Penitentiary. The maximum security prison had had no law library, no way for prisoners to learn about their legal rights.

The warden hadn't cared that even convicted killers had the right to aid in their own appeals. Jefferson James hadn't been just the prison warden. He'd been the judge, at least the appeals court judge, the jury and, more often than not, the executioner.

But Jed was no longer in any danger from Warden James. The warden was the one behind bars now. So Jed focused on what was truly important—on what had kept him going for the past three years.

"Did you find anything that will prove I was framed?" And who the hell had done it?

A sigh rattled the already crackling connection. "Not yet. But I will."

Jed appreciated the agent's support but there was only so much the man could do. "You don't even know where to start."

"You do," Rowe surmised. "That's why you broke out of prison."

"The prison broke," Jed reminded him. From the gunfire and explosions, the brick, mortar and wood structure had nearly imploded. "It was more dangerous to stay than to leave."

"Not now. It's too dangerous for you on the outside," the DEA agent insisted, his voice deep with a life-and-death urgency. "You need to let me handle this."

Over the past three years, Jed had learned that his black-and-white code of integrity was something few people followed. Most people, even law-enforcement officers, lived life with shades of gray. Some darker shades than others.

"Is there a shoot-on-sight order out on me?"

Rowe's silence confirmed Jed's suspicion.

The prison guard who had stepped aside and let him escape the burning ruins of Blackwoods had warned him that his life would be more at risk on the outside. That there were lawmen who took it very personally when one of their own was killed. Cop killers rarely survived in jail or on the outside.

"Then it's not safe for me to go back into custody, either," Jed pointed out. "No doubt I'd wind up having a fatal *accident*."

"*I* will bring you in," the DEA agent said. "And I'll vouch for your innocence."

A smile tugged at Jed's lips. "Do you really think

anyone is going to take your word that I'm innocent just because your girlfriend says so?"

"She's not my girlfriend."

Jed's breath left his lungs in a whoosh of surprise. He had only seen Rowe Cusack once since helping the agent survive his undercover assignment at Blackwoods Penitentiary, but during that brief meeting in the midst of the riot, he had been able to tell that the guy had fallen hard for Jed's younger sister. "Is Macy all right?"

Because if Rowe had hurt her, the DEA agent would be seeing Jed again—but not to bring him back to prison.

"She's my fiancée now," Rowe said.

"You proposed?" The guy had fallen *really* hard.

"She's everything you told me she was," Rowe said, his voice gruff with emotion, "and so much more. I would have been a fool if I let her get away."

Jed had been a fool like that once. He'd fallen hard but had let the woman get away. In the end, it had cost him his freedom. And given that shoot-on-sight order, it could wind up costing him his life, too.

"I hope she wasn't a fool to accept," Jed said. As he'd learned, people weren't always what you thought they were or what your heart wanted them to be.

"Your sister is no fool," Rowe said, defending her, his voice sharp with anger now.

"No," Jed agreed. Macy was the only one who had believed in his innocence…until the DEA agent. But Jed suspected that Rowe just believed in Macy, which was fine with him. His younger sister deserved to have someone who supported her and who obviously loved her. "Congratulations."

"If I had my way, she would already be my wife,"

Rowe admitted, "but she won't set a date for our wedding until your name is cleared."

Jed choked on a laugh. "So Macy's given you some incentive to help me."

"You gave me the incentive—when you saved my life," Rowe reminded him. "Twice."

"I didn't do that to give you incentive," Jed said. "I did it because it was the right thing to do." And because he could never have lived with himself had he let an innocent man be murdered.

"I know," Rowe said. "That's why I believe you. That's why I want you to do the right thing now. Tell me where you are, so I can bring you in."

Jed blew out a breath that steamed up the cracked Plexiglas of the old pay-phone booth. He'd already talked to the agent too long, just hopefully not long enough for the man to have tracked Jed's location. "Tell my sister I love her."

"If you love her, you would—"

"Stay alive. That's what Mace wants most of all," Jed said with absolute certainty, "my safety." Macy would have broken him out of prison herself if he'd agreed to go along with her plan. But he hadn't wanted her to risk her freedom for his. And for years he had believed that justice would prevail and his innocence would be proven—the real killer finally caught.

He wasn't that idealistic and naïve anymore. He knew that he was the only one who could prove his innocence. "I won't be safe until I have irrefutable proof that I killed no one."

Yet. Because he couldn't trust the justice system to work, he might have to take his own justice.

"Jed, you have to come back, or it won't matter if you clear your name," Rowe said, trying to reason with him.

But no one really understood that *nothing* mattered to Jed but clearing his name. Not even his own life…

"I'll keep in touch, Rowe."

Jed hung up, hopefully before Rowe had had time to trace his call. The DEA agent would excuse his interference as help. But Jed didn't need anyone's help. He had broken out of prison because there were certain things—certain *people*—only *he* could handle.

Erica Towsley was one of those people. He wadded up the page he had ripped from the dangling phone book and shoved it into the pocket of his jeans. He had found her. For over three years he'd had his lawyer looking for her to no avail. In the three days since he had escaped from Blackwoods Penitentiary, Jed had tracked down his alibi.

He stepped out of the booth and sucked in a breath as the wind picked up, whipping icy chunks of snow at him. But then he thought of *her,* and his blood heated. Oblivious to the freak late-spring snowstorm, he trudged along the deserted street deeper into the heart of the small town. The businesses were closed, the storefronts dark. But above a few of those businesses, lights glowed in some of the apartments on the second and third stories.

Behind the blinds at one of those windows, a shadow moved. He couldn't see any more than a dark, curvy silhouette, but his pulse quickened and his breath shortened.

He knew it was her.

ERICA SHIVERED BUT NOT because of the cold air seeping through the worn frames of the front windows. She shivered at what she saw as she gazed through the slats of the blinds.

Despite it being spring for a few weeks now, winter had snuck back into Miller's Valley in the form of a blizzard. But the return of winter wasn't what chilled her blood even with the snow blowing outside, nearly obscuring the street below the third-floor apartment. Nearly.

Erica still caught a glimpse of someone standing on the sidewalk across the street. He was just a tall, broad-shouldered shadow. But she could feel his gaze as he stared up at her window. And it chilled her far more than the cold air.

"There is no way that he found you," she whispered, reassuring herself again, like she had been doing since that special report three nights ago. Nothing was in her name. Not the business. Not the building. Not even the car she drove. "It's safe here."

But despite all of her assurances, those doubts niggled at her, jangling her already frazzled nerves. That was why she was up so late, because every creak and clunk of the old building had her pulse jumping and heart racing.

Even though her eyes were gritty and lids heavy, sleep eluded her. So she paced and kept watch, making sure those creaks and clunks were nothing but weather testing the structure of the old building.

But what about the shadow watching her window? She stepped closer but caught no glimpse of him now. Had there really been someone there, or had her overwrought nerves conjured up the image? She studied the street for several more moments, but the wind picked up, swirling the snow around and obliterating whatever footprints might have been on the street or sidewalk.

The snowstorm was late in the spring even for Michigan's unpredictable April weather. The temperatures had dropped, and rain had turned to sleet and then snow. No one would be out walking in such a storm.

She must have just imagined someone watching her. She exhaled a shaky breath of relief. As her nerves settled, exhaustion overwhelmed her. Maybe she could finally sleep. She stepped back from the window and crossed the living room to shut off the light switch by the door before heading down the hall.

Bam!

Her heart slammed into her ribs. This was no creak or clunk.

Bam! Bam! Bam!

Midstep, she stopped in the hall and whirled back toward the door that rattled under a pounding fist. Her hand trembling, she reached out and flipped on the lights as if the light alone would banish the monsters that had crept out of the shadows.

"Who's there?" she called out, her voice quavering as her nerves rushed back and overwhelmed her. She couldn't move—couldn't even step close enough to the dead-bolted door to peer through the peephole—as if he might be able to grab her through the tiny window.

"Ms. Towsley," a gruff voice murmured through the door, "I'm an agent with the Drug Enforcement Administration."

How the hell did he know who she was? And what could he possibly want with her? She knew nothing about narcotics; she rarely even remembered to take her vitamins.

"Prove it," she challenged him.

She shook off the nerves, so that she had the courage to press her eye to the peephole. But the man was so tall that he blocked most of the light in the hall. And he stood so close to the door that Erica couldn't see his face, only his wide chest.

"What?" he asked with an impatient grunt.

"Prove that you are who you say you are." Because she had been fooled before; she had thought a man was something he wasn't, and the mistake could have cost her everything.

Now she had even more to lose…

"Open the door," he replied, "and I'll show you my credentials."

"Just hold your ID up to the peephole," she directed him.

She had once chuckled over Aunt Eleanor installing the tiny security window in the door—given that no one had ever committed a crime in Miller's Valley. But now she was grateful for her great aunt's paranoia; too bad it had actually been the first symptom of the Alzheimer's that had eventually taken the elderly woman's life.

The shadows shifted as he stepped back and finally she was able to see—but just the identification the man held up: Rowe Cusack, Special Agent with the Drug Enforcement Administration. He was the lawman the news hadn't stopped talking about since the prison break. He was the DEA agent who had gone undercover to expose the corruption at Blackwoods Penitentiary and had nearly lost his life.

"Why are you here?" she asked.

What possible business could a DEA agent have in Miller's Valley? Fear clutched her stomach, tying it into knots. Perhaps this wasn't about drugs at all but about whom he'd met on that last assignment of his at Blackwoods.

"I need to talk to you about Jedidiah Kleyn," he said. His voice was raspy and gruff—just as it had been when he'd made his brief replies to the reporters' incessant questions.

She fumbled with the dead-bolt lock and opened the door. "Do you think he's looking for me?"

The man stepped inside and shoved the door closed behind himself. "He's not looking for you."

His dark eyes narrowed, he stared down at her—his gaze as cold as the snow melting on his mammothly wide shoulders. Dark stubble clung to his square jaw. "Not anymore."

Her heart slammed against her ribs as she realized her mistake. Once again she had fallen for this man's lies.

"He's found you," Jedidiah Kleyn said.

Erica had let a killer into her home. And now she was probably going to become his next victim...

Chapter Two

Despite having sworn that she wouldn't watch the news anymore, Macy Kleyn couldn't look away from the television screen. But the reporters or, worse yet, the mug shot from when Jed had been arrested weren't on the TV. The man whose face filled the screen was devastatingly handsome with a strong jaw, icy blue eyes and golden-blond hair.

But she didn't have to watch the news to see him. All she had to do was glance over to where he sat at a desk in a corner of his open apartment. It was what he was saying to the reporters gathered for that prerecorded press conference that held her attention.

"Jedidiah Kleyn is not the dangerous convict that earlier reports are claiming," he said, his deep voice vibrating in the TV speakers. "If not for Mr. Kleyn, I would not have made it out of Blackwoods Penitentiary alive. He saved my life, not once, but twice."

Macy's breath caught, but she released it in a shuddery sigh of relief. She would never be able to thank her big brother enough for saving the man she loved. But proving Jed's innocence would be a great place to start. If she had ever been able to figure out where to start...

"Are you suggesting that three years in prison reformed him?" a disembodied voice asked from behind the camera.

Rowe snorted. "Blackwoods reforms no one. Three years incarcerated there would have broken a lesser man than Jedidiah Kleyn."

"You seem to have an awful lot of respect for a cop killer," another disembodied voice, this one full of derision, remarked.

"That's not a question," Rowe pointed out. "But I'll answer it anyway. I don't believe Jedidiah Kleyn is guilty of the crimes of which he was convicted. And I intend to prove his innocence."

"Is that because Kleyn saved your life or because you're dating his sister?"

The screen went black, the speakers silenced instead of vibrating with his sexy voice. So she turned toward the real man.

"Thank you," she said.

"I'm not doing it for you," he replied, as he tossed the remote onto the couch and turned back to his laptop.

She crossed the room to his desk and leaned over him. Pressing against his back, she rested her head on one of his broad shoulders. His soft hair tickled her cheek, making her tingle.

Everywhere.

She caught just a glimpse of his laptop screen before he snapped it shut. "GPS?" Hope quickened her pulse almost as much as being close to her fiancé had. "Did you find him?"

Rowe shook his head. "He terminated the call before I could pinpoint his location."

"But you found out something," she surmised.

He opened up the screen again and pointed to the number on it.

"There aren't enough digits," she said, her hope dashed.

"No," her fiancé admitted, but he didn't sound as defeated as she felt. "But the area code and first few digits indicate that he called from a pay phone."

"Pay phone?"

He turned his face slightly toward her, his lips curving into a slight grin. "Apparently they still exist."

"And you can track it down?"

"Yes. But that number—well, the digits we have of that number—is registered to several phones in rural areas surrounding Grand Rapids."

"Rural?" Pay phones in farm towns? Maybe it made sense given that there were fewer towers and poorer cell reception.

Rowe shrugged. "Maybe he's hiding somewhere in the countryside..."

The sick feeling in her stomach convinced her otherwise. "We both know Jed didn't break out of prison to hide," she said. "My brother isn't hiding."

She suspected that he actually wanted to be found. Not by authorities but by the person who had framed him.

After a slight hesitation, Rowe said, "He's trying to clear his name."

"You don't believe that's all he's doing."

"Do you?" Rowe asked. He spun his chair around and tugged her down so that she straddled his hard thighs. His hands cupped her face, tipping up her chin so that their gazes met.

"No," she admitted. "If I had been framed for something I didn't do, I'd want justice." Even if she had to dole it out herself...

But did her brother want justice or revenge?

Jed could kill her—for everything she had cost him: his freedom, his reputation, his heart…

But despite her duplicity, she still looked beautiful to him. She had the pale golden hair of an angel; it shimmered even in the dim light of the antique chandelier dangling from the high ceiling of her apartment. And her eyes were a bright clear blue—wide now with fear. With her delicate features and flawless skin, she looked so young and innocent.

Where were the lines of guilt and stress? Where was the regret for what she had done to him? Was she so heartless that she had never given him another thought after she'd so callously destroyed his life?

"You're impersonating a government agent," she accused him, gesturing toward the badge Jed had lifted off Rowe Cusack when he had saved the DEA agent during the prison riot.

With a twinge of guilt, he slid it back into the pocket of his jeans. Rowe hadn't mentioned it, so he probably hadn't realized that Jed was the prisoner who had stolen it from him. The riot had been so chaotic and dangerous that the man had, no doubt, been more concerned about his life than his badge.

"That's the least of the charges I'm facing," Jed pointed out. "Thanks to you."

"Me?" Her voice cracked with emotion, and she stepped back, as if cowering from him in fear. "I had nothing to do with any of the things you've done."

"You had everything to do with it."

She shook her head. "No…"

He followed her, closing the distance between them. "Why did you do it?"

For three years that question had nagged at him. He could not figure out what her motivation had been.

Greed? Revenge? Once he had thought her too sweet and innocent for either emotion, but he'd had three years to realize how wrong he'd been about her.

"Wh-what did I do?" she asked, as if she really didn't know.

He chuckled at her attempt to feign innocence. But then those looks of an angel had probably always let her get away with her misdeeds. No one would ever suspect how devious she really was. "You set me up, sweetheart."

He had once called her sweetheart and meant it; he had been such a fool. "What did you get out of it? Money?"

If she had, she hadn't spent it on this place. There were cracks in the plaster ceiling and walls, and the hardwood floors were worn. The curtains even fluttered at the windows, as if the cold air blew right through the thin panes of glass.

He moved closer, trapping her between his body and the wall she had backed up against. "Revenge?"

He'd thought that she had understood why he'd had to break up with her before he left for Afghanistan. It wouldn't have been fair to expect her to wait for him, especially when there had been a strong possibility that he might not even return.

But he shouldn't have worried about her; she definitely hadn't waited for him. When he had come back home after his year-long deployment, she had already been wearing another man's ring.

"Revenge?" She echoed his question. "What are you talking about?"

"I don't know," he admitted. She hadn't seemed to care enough about his dumping her to want revenge on him. But then they hadn't been going out long when he'd received his deployment orders, calling him from the reserves back into active duty. "I don't know why you did it."

"Did what?" she asked, her brow furrowing with confusion.

Jed leaned down, so that his forehead nearly touched hers. "I don't know why you helped frame me for murder. Or was it all your idea?"

From having once interviewed her for a job, he knew her educational background and IQ. She was more than smart enough to have masterminded the embezzlement, murders and frame-up herself. And he wasn't the only man on whom she might have wanted revenge.

She gasped, and her breath was warm against his face. "I didn't. I had nothing to do with those murders."

Jed eased back to study her beautiful face. No wonder she had fooled him into falling for her lies and for her; she was a damn good actress because she nearly had him believing she wasn't involved. And he knew better.

"You had to be in on it," he insisted. "Or you would have come forward when I was arrested. Instead you disappeared."

She shook her head, tumbling her blond hair around her slender shoulders. In a bulky wool sweater, she looked so small and fragile. But he wouldn't let her looks deceive him again.

"I didn't disappear," she protested. "My aunt Eleanor's health was failing, so I came home to take care of her."

"My lawyer couldn't find you." And Jed had told the man that she might have returned to Miller's Valley where she'd grown up with her great aunt.

Her brow furrowed again. "Mr. Leighton definitely found me. I talked to him."

"No..."

Marcus Leighton wouldn't have lied to him. He was more than Jed's defense lawyer; he'd been his fraternity brother, too. And his friend.

"If he found you, he would have made you come forward." And provide the alibi that would have cleared Jed of all the charges against him.

"Mr. Leighton didn't want me to testify," she said, "because my testimony would only make you look guiltier."

Now he knew she was the one lying. He chuckled at her weak attempt to fool him. "I was with you during the murders. Your testimony would prove my innocence. You were my alibi."

Her face flushed bright red, but she shook her head again in denial. "I can't testify to what I can't remember."

"What the hell...? You're claiming amnesia?" There was no way Marcus would have believed that, and if he'd put her on the stand, the jury would have realized she was lying, too. Why hadn't Marcus put her on the stand if he'd actually found her?

"I was drugged," she said. "And I have the test results to prove it. I don't remember that night."

No matter how hard he'd tried over the past three years, he hadn't been able to forget that night. Or her...

How could she claim to remember none of it?

"So if using me was part of your plan, it didn't work," she said, anger replacing the fear in her eyes as she glared up at him. "I can't alibi you."

"You're lying." She had to be, otherwise he had lost his one hope of proving his innocence.

"Why would I lie?" she asked.

That was the question that had nagged at him.

Why?

A board creaked behind him, alerting him to someone else's presence. Had he been set up again?

He grabbed Erica, wrapping one arm around her waist and his other around her neck, so he could threaten to snap it if her backup had a weapon. Then he whirled toward the intruder.

And pain clutched his heart with all the force of a gunshot. But he hadn't been shot; he'd just been shocked by the appearance of the child who stumbled down the hall, wiping sleep from her dark eyes.

"Don't hurt her," Erica pleaded in an urgent whisper. "She's just a baby."

The child was actually two—probably almost three years old. She blinked and stared blearily up at him and Erica.

"Mommy?"

"Sweetheart, you need to go back to bed," Erica said, her voice tremulous despite her obvious efforts to sound calm and reassuring.

The little girl's lips pursed into a pout. "I wanna a drink," she stubbornly insisted.

Suddenly aware of how tightly he held her, Jed dropped his arms from around Erica's delicate frame. "You can get her the drink." He pitched his voice lower, so only she could hear him. "I won't hurt her."

Erica glanced from him to her daughter and back, obviously reluctant to leave him alone with her child.

But this kid was his, too. She was the spitting image of his sister, Macy.

Erica must have taken him at his word because she left the little girl standing in front of him. But the refrigerator was only steps away, through an open arch-way. Erica watched him carefully as she backed into the kitchen.

He dropped to his knees in front of the little girl and asked, "How old are you?"

Her chocolate-brown eyes widened as she studied him. She was as fearful as her mother had seemed of him. But his size had even intimidated violent criminals enough that during his three years in one of the most dangerous prisons in the United States, not very many inmates had been brave enough to try to mess with him. So of course he was going to scare a small child.

But she lifted her pointy little chin, as if forcing her-self to be brave, which made her even more like his feisty kid sister. Then she held up two fingers.

"You're two years old?"

"I'll be thrwee soon," she replied with a slight lisp, like the one his sister had had until the speech therapist their parents hired had corrected it.

His parents had constantly been hiring specialists to *fix* Macy, so that she could be as *perfect* as they had considered their firstborn: him. But he had only been perfect until he had been charged with double homi-cide; then they had stopped considering him their son entirely. They'd forgotten all about him just as Erica had apparently tried to forget him.

"What's your name?" he asked the child.

"Isobel," she replied. "What's yours?"

Dad. I'm your father.

Sure, Erica had been engaged before that night she'd spent with him—the night she claimed not to remem-ber. But Isobel was not Brandon Henderson's daughter, or she would have been blue-eyed and blond-haired like both her parents.

Instead she shared his coloring and looked exactly like his sister. She even sounded like Macy had at her age. Jed didn't need a DNA test; he was certain. But before he could open his mouth to utter anything, Erica interrupted.

"Here's your water, sweetheart!" She pressed a sippy cup into her daughter's small hand and lifted the child into her arms. "Now let me tuck you back into bed."

Jed could have vaulted to his feet and stopped her from carrying the child off down the hall. His reflexes were quick or he wouldn't have survived three years at Blackwoods, not to mention his tour in Afghanistan.

But he let them go.

Then he slowly drew in deep breaths, steadying his racing pulse. The apartment was small, so he overheard their conversation, no matter how softly they spoke.

"Who is that man?" the little girl asked her mother. "What's his name?"

"Jed," Erica replied.

"But who is he?" The little girl persisted as stubbornly as she had demanded her now-forgotten glass of water. "I never seen him 'fore. And he's so big."

"He's just a friend," Erica murmured. And he was surprised she didn't choke on her lie.

But that proved just how consummate a liar she was. She was obviously lying about not remembering that night, and now he had the proof. No matter what she claimed about her child, he knew the truth.

He had a daughter.

So whoever had framed him, obviously with Erica's help, hadn't just stolen years of Jed's life. He had lost precious years of Isobel's life, as well. He had missed his daughter being born, taking her first steps, uttering her first words…

Somehow, that person would have to pay for what he had taken from Jed.

THE BLACKWOODS COUNTY JAIL offered the same basic amenities that the prison once had—before it had been destroyed during the riot. Former warden Jefferson James had a cot on which to sleep. He went to the cafeteria for meals and a recreational area for entertainment. But what he'd just seen on television hadn't been entertainment, so he'd demanded to return to his cell.

The DEA agent continued to make Jefferson's life difficult. If only Kleyn had killed him, like Jefferson had ordered the inmate…

But instead of killing him, he'd helped the DEA agent escape Blackwoods. Now the DEA agent wanted to return the favor and prove Kleyn innocent of the crimes of which he'd been convicted. He probably was innocent—that was why he'd disobeyed Jefferson's order to kill. But his innocence made him even more dangerous to Jefferson. If proved unjustly convicted, his testimony would carry more significance. That was why he couldn't testify…

A shadow, sliced by the bars, fell across the floor in front of Jefferson. "You wanted to see me?"

No. He could barely look at Sheriff Griffin York. The young lawman was everything Jefferson despised—self-righteous, honorable and law-abiding as well as law-enforcing. But he did want to talk to the man.

"Took you damn long enough to get here," Jefferson griped.

"Kind of got my hands full cleaning up the mess from the riot," York bitterly remarked.

"Did you round up all the escapees yet?"

York's gaze hardened with resentment. "It's only been a few days."

"So you haven't apprehended any of them?"

"Some of them," the sheriff claimed and then goaded, "and some of your guards, as well. They're already talking. They have a lot to say about you."

Jefferson's lawyer wasn't worried about the testimony of coconspirators who had benefited from the crimes of which he was being convicted. It was Kleyn he worried about; he was the one who couldn't talk.

"What about the cop killer?" he asked. "He still at large?"

The sheriff's nostrils flared. "You don't need to worry about him."

Hope lifted Jefferson's spirit. "He's dead?"

"No. But his face is all over the news. He will be apprehended soon."

Jefferson didn't want him arrested. He wanted him dead. He had already put into motion the shoot-on-sight order; he just had to trust that someone else out there wanted Jedidiah Kleyn dead as badly as he did.

If the man had been framed, then the real killer would probably want to make sure Kleyn didn't live long enough to discover his identity...

HE'S OUT. HOW DID THE son of a bitch break the hell out of prison?

How had he survived it? How had he survived the year he'd spent in a war zone? Jedidiah Kleyn was some kind of superhero. Or he had been, until his shining armor had been permanently tarnished.

He grinned, his chest swelling with satisfaction in

accomplishing what he had barely considered possible. The perfect murder. Murders.

And the perfect revenge. Jedidiah Kleyn had lost everything.

But his life. Now it was time to take that, too.

Chapter Three

"I was wrong," a deep voice murmured. Jed spoke from where he stood in the hall, as if reluctant to step any closer to the child he had helped her conceive.

Erica stared down at her daughter's sleeping face. After a sip of water, the toddler had dropped immediately back into a deep slumber. The stranger hadn't unsettled or scared her like he had Isobel's mother. But that was because Erica knew him, although he wasn't the friend she'd told her daughter he was. If he had actually been a friend, she would have known him better; she would have known better than to trust him, let alone fall for him.

And even though he had been sentenced to spend two lifetimes in prison, Erica had known that this day would eventually come. She had known she would see Jedidiah Kleyn again. She stepped out of Isobel's room and closed the door.

He stared at it, though, as if he could see through the wood. As if he could see his child...

"You were wrong?" She prodded him for an explanation and a diversion. Hoping he would follow her, she led him away from her daughter, down the short hall and back into the living room.

She hadn't wanted to let him near her daughter. But

she hadn't wanted to scare the little girl either by showing her own fear. Some instinct, as well, had assured
Erica that no matter what else Jed might have done, he
wouldn't hurt a child.

"You're not my alibi," he agreed as he rejoined her
in the front room.

Finally he admitted it, banishing the doubts that had
plagued her for the past three years. What if his lawyer
had been wrong? What if Jedidiah hadn't committed
those heinous crimes? But Marcus Leighton had known
Jed far longer and better than she had. If his own friend
had believed he was guilty...

"Isobel's my alibi."

She gasped in surprise at his bizarre claim.

"She's irrefutable proof that I was with you that
night."

Anger surged through her, chasing away her fears.
She stepped close to him and stabbed his massive chest
with her fingertip. "She's irrefutable proof that I was
drugged and raped that night."

His neck snapped back as if she'd slapped him. "You
think I raped you?"

"You drugged me—"

"I did not drug you," he insisted with a weary-
sounding sigh. From the dark circles beneath his eyes,
she doubted he'd had any sleep since his escape. He had
probably spent every minute of that time tracking her
down. "I don't even believe you were drugged."

"Your lawyer has the lab results," she informed him.
"When I told him that my memory of that night was
cloudy, he had my blood drawn."

She should have known better than to believe, even
for a moment, that Jed might have actually cared about
her. Her own parents hadn't. She had been just a few

years older than Isobel was now when they'd dropped her off at her great aunt's with the promise that they would come back for her. Despite sending her cards and letters over the years that had reiterated that promise and renewed her hope, they had never come back.

"When was that?" he asked, his dark eyes intense.

She had to refocus on their conversation to realize what he was asking, but she still didn't understand why. "Three years ago, of course."

"No," he impatiently replied. "How many hours or days after we were together?"

Erica shrugged, wondering why he thought it mattered so much how many days or hours had passed. "I don't know. It was after you were arrested."

"So at least two days after that night?" he prodded her.

Would it have mattered how many days or hours? Her pulse quickened as she began to wonder and hope that she might not have been so wrong about him. Cautiously, she replied, "I guess."

He shook his head with disgust, as if he'd caught her in a lie. "If you had been drugged, it wouldn't have been in your system any longer."

"How do you know that?" she asked, her stomach tightening with dread.

She had hoped she was wrong about him; that he hadn't been the one responsible. But he seemed familiar with the drug she'd been slipped, probably in the water he'd given her at the office before she'd left with him that night.

He wouldn't have had to drug her to get her to go home with him. She had been so grateful, and relieved after a year of worrying, that he'd come back from

Afghanistan alive that she would have done anything
for him. And to be with him…

"Everyone knows that the drug you're talking
about—the one that erases your memory—doesn't stay
in your system very long," he said.

Growing up in Miller's Valley with her great aunt,
Erica had been sheltered. She knew nothing about
drugs. At her high school no one had used anything
more dangerous than marijuana.

"I didn't know that," she murmured, embarrassed by
her naïveté.

"I know you're lying," he said.

"I really didn't know—"

"You're lying about that night," he clarified. "I was
with you. I know you weren't drugged. You were just
upset after catching Brandon with another woman."

That hadn't upset her. Brandon Henderson hadn't
even been her real fiancé; he had just been too stubborn
and too arrogant to accept her no to his proposal. So he
had insisted she think about it and wear his ostentatious
diamond ring while she did. When Jed had returned
from Afghanistan, she had realized why. Brandon had
wanted to stick it to the friend he had always envied
and resented. That was why she had gone into Brandon's office the night the man had been murdered—to
tell him where to go with his ring.

"I was upset," she agreed. But not for the reasons Jed
thought. She'd been upset that she had let Brandon use
her to hurt him. But then Jed had used her, too, and far
worse than Brandon had.

After being a pawn in their sick, deadly game, she
had realized that she should have stayed in Miller's
Valley. It was much safer for her here. So even if her

neighbor hadn't called to warn her about her great aunt's deteriorating health, she would have come home.

But Marcus Leighton had always known where she was. Why had he lied to Jed?

Had he lied to her, too?

If Jed's rage was out of control, as his friend had claimed, wouldn't he have killed her already for not coming forward with the alibi he'd planned? But he had yet to lay a hand on her. Her pulse quickened at the thought of him touching her. Again.

"I took you back to my place," Jed said. "You remember that, don't you?"

"I remember you threatening to kill Brandon for hurting me," she replied.

"His girlfriend remembered me threatening him, too," he said with a sigh. "And she testified to it in court. She also claimed that she left me and Brandon alone together."

Doubts began to niggle. She hadn't heard that testimony. But she hadn't gone to court. Leighton hadn't wanted her there. And she had needed to be with her aunt in Miller's Valley. She had followed news reports, though, but must have missed the day the girlfriend had testified.

"You and I both know she lied," Jed said, "that you and I left *her* alone with him. You could have testified to that even if you really don't remember what else happened."

"I don't remember..." But heat warmed her face at the lie. She didn't remember everything, but images flashed through her mind. Images of the two of them, naked and wrapped tightly in each other's arms.

"You're lying again," he accused her, his voice sharp with frustration.

"I remember that you took me back to your place," she admitted.

"It was close to the office, and I didn't want you driving, as upset as you were."

She remembered that, too, and that she had been mad, so mad that the anger had made her light-headed and unsteady enough that Jed had carried her up the steps of his loft to his bedroom. Then when Marcus Leighton had told her she'd been drugged, she had realized it hadn't been the anger that had affected her like that.

"Just rest," Jed had told her, as he'd leaned down to press a kiss to her forehead.

But she'd grabbed his hand. She'd stopped him from leaving her. And she suspected she would have done that even if she hadn't been drugged.

"You remember more than that," he challenged her, as he studied her face.

It had to be flushed because her skin was hot and tingling.

"You know I didn't rape you," he said, leaning down so that his mouth was mere inches from hers. "You wanted me..."

She swallowed hard, unable to deny her desire. "I was a fool."

"Is that why you didn't come forward?" he asked, his brow furrowing in confusion. "Because you were too embarrassed?"

"I went to your lawyer," she told him again. "Mr. Leighton said—"

"Forget Marcus for now," he said as if he couldn't deal with the possibility that his friend might have betrayed him. "Why didn't you go to the police?" he asked. "I told the investigating detectives about you, but they didn't believe that I really had an alibi. Did they even talk to you?"

She shook her head, and sympathy tugged at her that no one had believed him. But his sister...

The news crews had relentlessly hounded Macy Kleyn, ridiculing her for supporting a cop killer. The young woman had always staunchly defended her brother's innocence.

Had he been innocent?

"Why didn't you go to the police?" He repeated his question.

"I didn't know if my testimony would help you or hurt you," she explained. Because even then, despite what his lawyer had said, she'd had doubts about his guilt. But she'd written those doubts off as pride that she hadn't wanted to have been so wrong about the man for whom she'd fallen. "And Marcus was adamant that it would hurt you."

"How?"

"It would have shown premeditation. The prosecutor would have said that you drugged me to provide yourself with an alibi." He had used her, just as his friend had in their rivalry against each other. But, as Marcus Leighton had said, Jed had taken their sick rivalry too far. "Once I passed out, you left me and returned to the office and killed Brandon. With as close as your apartment was to the office, you had plenty of time."

"Plenty of time to bludgeon him to death, carry him down to the parking garage, put his body into his car and set it ablaze?" Jed fired the questions at her as if he was the lawyer, and she was the one on trial. "Oh, and kill the police officer who caught me burning the dead body?"

"It's possible..." *Wasn't it?*

He shook his head. "I made love to you all night." His voice dropped even lower so that it was just a rough whisper as he added, "Over and over again."

Those images flitted through her mind again—their naked bodies intimately entwined, their mouths fused together. Their hearts beating in the same frantic rhythm. So many images had haunted her over the past few years, staying as vivid as if they'd just made love hours—not years—ago.

Would he have had time to commit those horrific crimes and make love to her so thoroughly?

"*I* never left you," he insisted. "You left me."

"I left you that morning," she admitted. When she had awakened in his bed, in his arms, she'd slipped out of his loose grasp and hurriedly dressed. She hadn't been able to believe what she'd done—how she'd given in to her desires to spite her pride. After he'd dumped her before leaving for Afghanistan, she never should have trusted him with her body or her heart. "But you'd left me first—more than a year before."

"I got deployed."

"You left me before you got deployed," she reminded him. "You didn't want me waiting for you." And, haunted by all the years she'd spent waiting for someone she loved to come back for her, she had readily agreed to end their budding relationship even though—or maybe because—she had already fallen for him.

"We'd only gone out a few times before I got called back to active duty," he reminded her. "I couldn't ask you to wait for me."

"Yes, you could have." Then, even if she hadn't been able to agree to wait, she would have at least known that he cared about her, too. "But you told me that you didn't see us working out anyway. That we weren't really compatible."

And she had believed him…until she'd seen his face when he had returned and found her in Brandon's office, wearing his ring. She had been trying to give it back that day, too. She'd only gone out with his business partner a few times over the year Jed had been gone, and mostly just so she could ask about Jed. So she had been using Brandon as a connection to the man she really wanted. That was why she had let him talk her into wearing that ring to think about his proposal—because she'd felt guilty.

"I was lying then," Jed said.

"I didn't know that. I believed that you really didn't see any future for us," she said. And that was why she had felt like a fool when she'd awakened in his arms. What if he'd only been jealous of his friend and hadn't really cared about her at all? Because if he had, how had he dropped her so easily?

Just as easily as her parents had dropped her at Aunt Eleanor's and never returned despite all their promises…

"Is that why you didn't come forward to offer me an alibi?" he asked. "Because you wanted revenge over my dumping you before I left for Afghanistan?"

She sucked in a breath. Apparently he didn't think very highly of her at all. When he'd told her that he saw no future for them, he must have been telling the truth then. And he was lying now, to try to make her feel guilty enough to help him.

"I have told you," she said, "again and again that I did come forward. I talked to your lawyer."

Jed shook his head, once again rejecting her claim. "Marcus swore to me that he never found you."

"Then he lied."

And, she thought, if Marcus really had lied to his friend and former fraternity brother, he would have had no qualms about lying to a woman he had barely known. Had Marcus lied about everything? Jed's guilt? His violent temper?

After that first initial jolt of fear at realizing she had let Jed into her apartment, she hadn't remained afraid—if she had, she would have tried to get to the phone or she would have shouted for her neighbor to call the police. Of course she would have had to shout really loud for Mrs. Osborn to hear her, but the elderly lady definitely would have come to her aid.

But instinctively she had known that she was in no real danger from Jed—that he wouldn't physically harm her or their daughter. He may have had reason to harm her, though, had she stupidly believed lies about him...

Jed's brow furrowed. "I don't understand...why would he lie?"

"He thought you were guilty," she divulged. "He said that Afghanistan changed you—that you came back so angry and violent."

A muscle twitched along his jaw, as if he tightly clenched it—controlling that rage of which his friend had warned her. "Was I violent with you that night?"

"From what I remember...?" She bit her lip and shook her head. He had been anything but violent. He had definitely been passionate but gentle, too.

"So I didn't rape you."

"No, but I was drugged. I don't care if the results came too late. I know that something wasn't right that night. I felt dazed or drunk, and I'd had nothing but that water at the office." At the time, she'd thought it had just been the surrealness of finally making love with the man she had loved for so long and had worried that, because of his deployment, she would never have had the chance to be that close to him.

Jed nodded, almost as if he was beginning to accept that what she told him was the truth.

"My memory of that night is sporadic," she continued. "I can testify that I was with you that night, but I can't swear that you never left me. Your lawyer was right that I wouldn't have been a convincing alibi—that my testimony could have actually hurt you more than I could have helped you."

And that was why she hadn't gone to the police, despite the twinges of guilt she'd felt over staying silent. While she believed that a man should be punished for his crimes, she hadn't wanted to help dole out that punishment. Not to Jed—not given what he might have endured in Afghanistan.

According to his lawyer, there had been more than sufficient evidence for his conviction without her muddying the waters. But would she have muddied the waters, or had Leighton already done that?

His broad shoulders slumped, and his breath shuddered out in a ragged sigh. "I spent all these years thinking that all I had to do to clear my name was find you."

"Is that really all you want?" To clear his name—not to kill her? If she could have been his alibi but hadn't come forward, she wouldn't blame him for wanting to harm her.

He glanced toward the hall down which was his daughter's room. "That *was* all I wanted."

"To clear your name?"

"I am innocent, Erica," he insisted, his voice and gaze steady with sincerity. "I didn't kill anyone. Not in Afghanistan and damn well not when I returned."

Guilt gripped her heart, making it ache. Had she been wrong? Had she stood by and done nothing while an innocent man rotted in prison? "But there was the witness—the one who actually saw you shoot the cop."

Jed shrugged. "He was a vagrant who hung out in the parking garage. He was usually drunk. His testimony shouldn't have held any weight."

"He didn't look like a vagrant in court. The jury believed him." And so had she.

"You followed the trial?"

Erica nodded. The judge had opened up the courtroom to news crews, which had covered and replayed every salacious detail of the trial. "But your lawyer told me how it would go before it even started. He knew the evidence against you was insurmountable, and that my testifying would only make you look guiltier, that it would help prove premeditation."

"Or your alibi might have given me reasonable doubt…"

Instead she had been the one with the doubts. But then, pretty much everyone she had ever loved had lied to her. Over and over again…

"Your lawyer showed me pictures of the crime scene, too." She shuddered. Because of the graphic nature of the images, the media hadn't been allowed to show crime-scene photos on the news. For years Erica had wished she had never seen them, either.

"Why would Marcus do that?" Jed asked.

"I don't know…" She hadn't understood any of it— the rivalry between men who were supposed to be friends and business partners or the lawyer being so certain that his client was guilty. She'd wondered then if Jed had actually confessed to his friend.

Jed's brow furrowed with lines of confusion. "It's as

if he was trying to convince you of my guilt when he was supposed to be doing everything in his power to prove my innocence."

"He didn't prove your innocence to a jury. He did a much better job of proving your guilt," she said, "at least to me."

Jed shook his head, as if trying to make sense of it all. "I thought he was my friend. He and Brandon and I all belonged to the same fraternity."

"Brandon wasn't really your friend," she pointed out.

Jed must have realized how much his former fraternity brother and business partner had envied and resented him. But then Brandon had been very good at hiding that resentment behind a façade of charm and humor—otherwise she never would have spent any time with him—not even to stay connected to Jed.

"And apparently neither was Marcus," Jed said with a heavy sigh. "So is he the one who framed me?"

Framed? The idea didn't seem all that preposterous anymore. In fact it seemed highly likely, which both relieved and sickened her.

"It would explain why he knew how much evidence there was against you—if he planted it." Just as he had planted the doubts in her muddled mind, so that she had done nothing when Isobel's father had gone to prison for a crime he hadn't committed. She should have at least talked to him, let him tell her his side of that night.

But she had worried that she would fall for his lies again.

What if she'd been wrong about him?

Her head pounded, and her stomach pitched as she realized the full impact of what she'd done...to Jed and their daughter. She had cost them three years together, and, from what she had seen on the news about the corruption at Blackwoods Penitentiary, she had nearly cost Jed his life.

"I can't believe Jed Kleyn got out," Marcus Leighton said, his hand shaking as he poured himself another drink.

"It was your job to make sure he stayed in prison for the rest of his life," the man with Marcus reminded his partner in crime.

But Marcus had never really been a partner, just a greedy ally. Not even so much an ally as a puppet, really. Easily manipulated. Too easily…

Marcus stared up at his companion, his eyes already clouded with confusion and drunkenness. "I'm not responsible for him breaking out of prison."

"He was supposed to die in prison." That had been how the plan—the brilliant plan—was to have concluded.

"He'd only been inside three years." Marcus was sober enough to remember. As if realizing that his brain was fogging, he pushed his glass aside. Alcohol sloshed over the rim and onto the case file lying on his mahogany desk. It was an antique, like most of the furnishings in the elegant office. Marcus enjoyed the finer things in life.

"Three years wasn't long enough." Jed wouldn't have suffered enough. Not yet. If he had lasted just a few more years, an inmate would have been rewarded—just as Marcus's ineptitude had been rewarded—for taking Jedidiah Kleyn's life.

But maybe this was a better and far more satisfying conclusion to his plan. Now he would get to take Jed's life himself—with his own hands. And he would be able to watch Jed's face while he did it.

"He'll be apprehended," Marcus said. "It doesn't matter how many other prisoners escaped during the riot, every cop is out there looking for Jed."

He shook his head. "You heard that DEA agent on the news, didn't you? The guy praises Kleyn for saving his life. He believes his claims of innocence."

Marcus's breath shuddered out. "That's why he asked for copies of all my records. He already got the police files and court transcripts."

His heart pounded a little faster. Marcus was so inept that he might have left something in those records that could lead back to *him*. "When is he coming for them?"

The color left Marcus's face, leaving him even pastier than the long Michigan winter had. "He's coming by tomorrow."

He had time. "Then we'll have to destroy them tonight."

Marcus nodded eagerly, and his shoulders slumped with relief. "Of course. Yes, we will."

The man really was an idiot, which made him a liability. "We'll have to get rid of any evidence leading back to me."

"To us."

"No, to me." He lifted his gun from beneath the edge of Marcus's desk. "Just like the evidence, you're going to get destroyed tonight, my friend."

It wouldn't matter who had begun to believe Jedidiah Kleyn's claims of innocence. He wouldn't be able to prove it. He wouldn't die a hero; he would die a killer.

And like Marcus Leighton, he would die soon. But first he would suffer so much that he would be almost grateful for death...

Chapter Four

Jed stood in the open doorway, casting a dark shadow over his sleeping daughter.

His daughter.

He had a child—one he would have never learned about had he not broken out of prison. Knowing *about* Isobel and now wanting to get to *know* Isobel made him even more determined to prove his innocence. But most of all he couldn't have her growing up with the stigma of everyone thinking her father was a killer. Or worse yet, with *her* thinking her father was a killer.

Because he wasn't.

Yet.

His skin prickled on the nape of his neck, and the muscles between his shoulder blades twitched. He was no longer alone with his daughter. After three years in one of the most dangerous prisons in the world and, before his incarceration, a year in Afghanistan, his instincts were finely honed. So honed that he didn't need to turn around to know that Erica had joined him. He could smell her—that sweet vanilla scent that reminded him of baking cookies and pies. And he could feel her as his skin tingled with the heat of awareness.

"I couldn't find the business card Marcus Leighton gave me," she said.

Regret tightened his guts. He didn't have any time to waste tracking down the Judas who'd betrayed him. Not only had Marcus not put Erica on the stand, but he'd convinced her that Jed was guilty.

Why?

Unlike Brandon, Marcus had always been a true friend to Jed. He hadn't been competitive with him; he'd actually seemed to be in awe of him—more fan than friend.

"But I looked him up online," Erica said, "and I found his address."

For the past few years he'd thought she had sold him out. But like him, she had been a victim, too. Along with the jury of twelve of his peers, she had believed the evidence that had been manufactured to prove his guilt.

Had Marcus manufactured that evidence? But he had no motive to frame Jed…unless he had been hiding his own guilt. Brandon Henderson and Marcus Leighton had not been friends. Brandon had bullied and harassed Marcus, as he had bullied and harassed everyone but Jed.

Jed had thought he only needed to find his alibi and make her come forward to prove his innocence. But Erica had raised valid points about her testimony. With the holes in her memory, she wouldn't be able to convince an appeals court that he hadn't left her alone in his bed that night, gone back to the office and committed the double murder.

No, the only way to prove his innocence beyond a shadow of anyone's doubt—the appeals court, Erica's and their daughter's—was to find the real killer. "Where is he?"

"I'm not going to tell you," she said.

Finally able to drag his gaze away from Isobel, he turned to Erica. She stood in the light from the hall, still looking like an angel, but from the firm set of her jaw and the hard gleam in her eyes, she intended to be as stubborn as the devil to keep the information he wanted from him.

Over the past few years, he had dealt with people far more stubborn than she could ever be. Like the warden of Blackwoods, who had been the very devil himself. Now Warden James was behind bars for all his criminal activities.

And Jed was out.

A bitter chuckle at the irony slipped through his lips, and he glanced back at Isobel, worried that he had awakened her.

"She sleeps like a rock," Erica assured him. "She doesn't hear anything when she's out."

"That's good," Jed said. "Then she won't hear me take your computer from you to look up Marcus's address."

He was *not* going back to prison to serve out his two life sentences; he had already served enough time for crimes he hadn't committed. Realistically, he would probably have to serve time for breaking out of prison, but he could accept the punishment for a crime he had committed.

"You don't need to look up his address," she said. "I'll drive you to his office."

"His office will be closed now." He gestured toward the darkness beyond Isobel's bedroom window. "And you're not driving me anywhere."

"He lives above his office," she explained, "in Grand Rapids. You'll need a ride there."

"I got here and buses don't run to Miller's Valley," he

reminded her. He didn't need a ride. And he definitely didn't want Erica with him when he questioned Marcus.

"So you stole a car, too?"

In addition to what? Murder? Did she still have her doubts? Was she not able to completely trust him? But wouldn't that make her more anxious to get rid of him than to want to go along with him?

"You can't leave Isobel here alone." And he wasn't about to take his daughter anywhere near a possible killer.

"My neighbor from across the hall is coming over to watch her," she said. "I told Mrs. Osborn that I have an emergency in Grand Rapids."

"You don't have anything in Grand Rapids," he said.

"I do." Hopefully his vindication. "Stay here with our daughter."

She shook her head, which swirled her golden hair around her slender shoulders.

He swallowed a groan, fighting his attraction to her. It didn't matter how damn beautiful she was; he couldn't trust her. He only really had her word that Marcus had lied to her. His friend deserved to give his side of the story before Jed entirely condemned him. Jed had known Marcus far longer and, he'd thought, better than he'd ever known Erica Towsley.

"I have questions only Marcus can answer," she said. "I want to hear, from his mouth, why he lied to me. And I want to know why he lied about you."

And, obviously, she didn't trust Jed enough to bring those answers back to her. But then she had spent the past few years convinced that he was guilty of murder. He was lucky she hadn't called the police instead of her neighbor.

A knock rattled the front door, and Jed's heart rattled

his rib cage with a sudden jolt of fear. What if she had called the police? What if she had only been playing him when she'd acted as if she was beginning to believe in his innocence?

"Open Isobel's window and go out the fire escape," Erica said, her soft voice pitched low with urgency.

"What— Why?"

"You can't let Mrs. Osborn see you," she explained. "She obsessively watches the news. She might recognize you from all the media coverage of the prison breakout."

The door rattled again.

"Go down the fire escape," she ordered him. "My car's the blue minivan parked below it in the alley. It's unlocked." Her blue eyes gleamed as she added, "I have the keys, though."

"I don't need your van," he reminded her.

He had one of his own parked in the very same alley. The black panel van had belonged to a guard, like the clothes that Jed had found packed in a suitcase in the back of it. The guard, one of the warden's henchmen, had obviously planned to flee before charges could be filed against him. But he hadn't made it out of the riot. Like a few others, he had died behind bars because of the crimes he'd carried out for the warden. He had tortured and killed the prison doctor who'd helped the DEA agent escape.

The death of the doctor, who so many of the inmates had loved, was what had inspired the riot. When he'd ordered Doc's murder, the warden had gone too far. He'd ordered Jed's death, too, but the riot had protected and eventually freed Jed. But even without Rowe's warning, he would have known that he was probably in more danger outside of prison than he'd ever really been in it.

At least he didn't need to worry about Warden James anymore...

"But you need Marcus Leighton's address," she reminded him.

"Fine. I'll wait for you," he assured her. He also waited before going out the window. Hiding in the dark shadows of Isobel's bedroom, he watched Erica walk down the hall toward the door.

Her hips, fuller than he remembered, swayed in her jeans. His guts tightened with desire. It wasn't fair that she was so damn beautiful...

"Thank you for coming," Erica said as she opened the door. "I'm sorry I woke you up."

"It's okay, honey," a female voice, gruff with sleep and possibly age, assured her. "I know that you would never do that unless you had an emergency. I hate the thought of you going out after dark, though—what with those escaped convicts on the loose. They're all armed and dangerous, you know."

"I'm sure the media is exaggerating that," Erica said, keys rattling as she grabbed her purse.

"No, honey, they're bad men—every last one of them. But that cop killer—he's the worst. I hope they catch him soon." A board creaked, as if the woman had moved down the hall.

Toward Isobel's bedroom.

If Jed didn't leave now, he might get caught. He pushed up the window and stepped onto the wrought iron of the fire escape. The wind rustled Isobel's curtains, so he pulled the window closed. Hopefully Erica would come back and lock it.

He hated the thought of leaving Isobel alone. The old woman sitting with her was no protection for the vulnerable child—not with a killer on the loose who had already tried to ruin Jed's life once. Harming his daughter would hurt Jed more than spending the rest of his life locked up.

But, hopefully, no one else knew about Isobel. While Erica claimed that his lawyer had always known her whereabouts, Marcus might not have realized she was pregnant. He had certainly never given Jed any hint that he had become a father.

But then he couldn't trust anything his lawyer had ever told him because he'd apparently kept much more from him than Jed had realized. Like the documents that might have helped Jed in his defense, if he'd been able to track down the funds that had been embezzled from his clients' accounts. If Marcus had lied about Erica, he might have lied about the warden denying Jed access to those documents.

Or was it Erica that he shouldn't trust? Maybe she had been working with Marcus. Maybe she was still working with the lawyer.

Maybe instead of driving Jed to Grand Rapids, she intended to drive him right to a police station...

COULD SHE TRUST JED? Erica studied his face in the glow of the dashboard lights. He had insisted on driving, his hands clamped tight around the steering wheel. His square jaw, shadowed with dark stubble, was also clamped tight—as if he fought to hold in his rage.

How much had that rage built up during three years in prison for crimes he hadn't committed? If he hadn't committed them...

Had she been a fool to so easily accept his claims of innocence? While she now remembered more of that night, of their making love again and again, she couldn't remember every minute of it. She couldn't swear that he had never left her...

"I didn't do it," he said, as if he had read her mind.

She jumped and knocked her knee against the dash, pain radiating up her leg. She had the passenger's seat pulled up close to it because the child booster seat was behind it and Isobel always kicked the back of it. "How did you know what I was thinking?"

She had never been able to truly tell what Jed had been thinking or feeling. So it wasn't fair if he could read her that easily...

"I figured you would start doubting my innocence again," Jed said. "After all, it would be easier for you if I was guilty."

"Easier?" Then she had willingly gone off alone with a killer. At least she had drawn him away from Isobel, though. At least she had kept her daughter safe...

But she remembered the look on Jed's face as he had stared down at their sleeping daughter. His jaw hadn't been rigid then. His dark eyes hadn't been hard. They had been soft and warm with awe and affection. He would never hurt Isobel.

"If I was really the killer, your conscience would be clear," he replied. "You wouldn't feel guilty for doing nothing while I was sent to prison."

"I explained why I did nothing." Except for the reasons she'd kept to herself, except for her personal baggage. She had never admitted to him that her parents had abandoned her with her great aunt. He had probably assumed she'd been an orphan—not unwanted.

A muscle twitched along his cheek. "Because of Marcus's lies."

He turned the van onto a cobblestone street and parked at the curb. At this hour there was no fight to get a meter. Every one of the metal meters stood guard over an empty parking spot.

"Are you sure this is the place?" he asked as he gazed up at the brick building, which was sandwiched between a restaurant and a bookstore.

"Yes," she confirmed, as she located the address on the building. The numbers on the brass plate matched the address she had found online.

A couple of lights glowed in the two stories above the ground-floor office. But lights glowed in the office windows, as well. At three o'clock in the morning, it was the only building with more illumination than just security lights.

"He was even written up in the Grand Rapids magazine about his renovation of this historic building," she said, remembering the article she had found online when looking for his address.

"He must have been more successful with other cases than he was mine," Jed murmured, "because it seems that since my incarceration, he certainly moved up in the world."

Erica hadn't found much else online about Marcus Leighton except his address and articles about his representing the cop killer, Jedidiah Kleyn. "I don't think he had any other high-profile cases, or they would have come up when I searched for his name on Google."

"If losing my case or, hell, just representing me, hurt his career, he didn't pay for this place with what I paid him." That look was back on Jed's handsome face, the intense rage that he was barely managing to control with a clenched jaw and flared nostrils.

Afghanistan may not have made him a violent man, but surely surviving three years in a prison as dangerous as Blackwoods Penitentiary had. If she hadn't insisted on coming along with him, she could not imagine what Jed might have done to Marcus Leighton to get the answers he wanted.

Erica wanted those answers, too. She reached for the door handle, but he leaned over and covered her hand with his. His skin was rough and warm against hers. Since it was spring, she had already packed away her gloves and winter gear. She wished she was wearing gloves now, not because of the unseasonable cold but because of how Jed's touch affected her. It brought all those images—of the two of them making love—rushing back to her.

"You should stay in the van," he said, leaning closer to her—so close that only inches separated his head from hers.

"No," she said. "I didn't come with you to just sit in the van."

She wasn't sure she would mind if he stayed in it with her, sitting so close that she could feel the heat of his heavily muscled body. But he didn't intend to stay with her; he was going to leave to go after his lawyer. She wasn't certain what his intentions were when confronting Marcus Leighton. And that was why she had insisted on coming along, to stop him from really becoming a killer.

"If he set me up for the reason I think he did, it's too dangerous for you to go in there with me." He glanced at the building. "I have a bad feeling about this."

"Because of the lights?" She wondered herself why so many of them were burning.

"Yeah, what's he doing up at this hour?" Jed asked, his eyes narrowed in suspicion as he stared up at the building. "It's almost like he knew I was coming. We could be walking into a trap."

She sucked in a breath as fear squeezed her lungs. But maybe he was just trying to scare her...

Jed turned back to her, his face still close as he leaned across her, his hand covering hers on the door handle. His eyes were so dark that she couldn't read the emotions swirling in them. But she almost believed one of them could be genuine concern for her safety.

Then she remembered where they were. "We're only a couple of blocks from the police department. Surely, no one would be bold enough to set up a trap here—where they could so easily be caught."

Or where Jed could so easily be caught. Maybe it was a trap.

"Erica..." He lifted his hand from hers to cup her cheek.

His touch had her skin tingling and nerves jangling. She had to get away from him and from all those feelings his touch brought back, so she pushed open the door and jumped out of the minivan. Before he could get around the front of the van, she was at the door to the office. It stood open, as if Marcus really had been expecting them.

Jed cursed beneath his breath as he joined her at the open door. "I don't have a weapon," he said, as he reached into his pocket. Instead of a gun, he drew out gloves and pulled them on, stretching the leather taut over his big hands. The gloves obviously weren't his any more than the wool jacket, which was too tight in the shoulders, was. "So I can't protect you."

She doubted that Jed really needed a weapon to protect himself or her. All he needed was his size and his muscle. But then that wouldn't be very effective against bullets.

"You have to stay out here," he insisted.

Maybe he was right. She had no protection against bullets, either. And she trusted that he wouldn't let her get hurt. If he had wanted her dead, he could have killed her at any point in the past few hours. If she went inside with him, though, and he lost control of the rage that boiled within him, she wanted to calm him and prevent the lawyer from getting hurt.

There was no telling what he might do if she let him go inside alone.

And if something had already happened inside, wouldn't the lights be off? Would a killer wait for them with all the lights burning?

She shook her head, unwilling to be left behind. "Jed—"

But he had his own argument for her to stay outside, one she couldn't fight. "Our daughter needs her mother."

She shivered as snow began to whirl around them, a cold wind whipping up the powder that already lay on the ground, and tossing around the falling flakes. She nodded, as if she intended to wait.

But he was inside for only a minute or two when she slipped through that open door and down the hall to where the lights burned on the first floor. She passed through a dark reception area to the open door to what must have been Leighton's office.

She followed him because their daughter needed her father, too. The little girl had already been denied him too long.

But it wasn't just for Isobel that Erica had gone after Jed. Like Jed, Erica wanted to know why he had been framed. Actually, she wanted to know if he had been framed. But she didn't intend to use violence to find the answers to all her questions and doubts.

Her muscles paralyzed with horror, she froze in the doorway—unable to move, unable to believe what she was seeing. She hadn't seen anything as gruesome since the lawyer had showed her those crime-scene photos.

Marcus Leighton was already dead. He was slumped in his chair, his shirt red with his own blood—his eyes open in shock.

ONE MAN DEAD. ONE TO GO.

He had no illusions that Jedidiah Kleyn would be as easy to kill as Marcus Leighton had been. If Kleyn was that vulnerable, he would have already been dead. He wouldn't have survived Afghanistan.

And he damn well wouldn't have survived Blackwoods Penitentiary. But he was in more danger out here, especially if he showed up at Leighton's office and stepped into the trap left for him.

While he had left the door open, he had reengaged the alarm. Once someone crossed the threshold, a call would be placed to the local police department.

As close as the office was to the police station, there was no way Jed would escape if he were the one to trip the alarm. Once police officers discovered the escaped convict standing over a dead body, they would assume the worst, and they would react accordingly—with bullets.

But if Jed hadn't yet figured out Marcus's betrayal and someone else set off the alarm, a contingency plan was already in place—thanks to what he'd discovered in Marcus's files.

He actually hoped that Jed didn't spring the trap he

had set at Marcus's office. Because the contingency plan would be a much more painful end to Jedidiah Kleyn than going out in a blaze of gunfire.

Chapter Five

A gasp had Jed's muscles tightening in apprehension. That breath hadn't come from the body; Marcus Leighton was dead. Jed had checked his pulse to confirm death. The man's skin was already cold. And so was Jed's blood—cold with dread.

He turned toward the door and found Erica watching him—her eyes as wide with shock and horror as Marcus's. She obviously thought Jed had killed his lawyer. He shook his head in denial of the question she hadn't even bothered to ask. She had just assumed his guilt, not even looking around as he had, for the real killer.

No one else was inside the building; it was just the two of them. And the dead man.

"He was shot." Jed pointed to the hole in Leighton's chest, burned through his blood-soaked shirt. He lifted his palms. "I don't have a gun."

With a trembling hand, Erica pointed to the one sitting across the desk from the body. Leighton must have been visiting with someone who'd pulled the Glock 9 mm gun on him, shot him and then left it on the desk next to the half-empty glass of liquor. So whoever had shot the lawyer was someone he had known well enough to drink around. Back in the frat house, Marcus had discovered that he was a cheap and sloppy drunk, and so he'd learned to only imbibe around people he could trust.

"You think Marcus handed me the gun to shoot him with?" He snorted at her suspicion. "Touch him. He's already cold. I did not kill him."

But the fact that she automatically thought he had shot Marcus told him what he needed to know: Erica would never trust that he wasn't a killer. Maybe not even after he found the real killer...

It wasn't Marcus.

He hadn't sold out Jed to hide his own guilt. He'd just sold him out for money.

Jed gazed around the office with its mahogany paneled walls. Filing cabinets had been built right into the walls, beneath rows of shelves. Jed reached for one of the handles, grateful that he wore gloves—ones he'd found in the guard's vehicle. He closed his fingers around a brass handle, pulling open a drawer to search for his records.

He pulled open drawer after drawer until he found the *K* section—or where the *K* section should have been. All the records under *K* were gone. Before he could search elsewhere in the office, a noise caught his attention.

His muscles tightened at the distant wail of a police car. Just like the last murder, this one was probably also a setup.

If the killer had called the police to report his crime, he hadn't left any evidence for Jed to find. Undoubtedly there was nothing in the office that would lead back to the real culprit. Like last time, it would probably all lead to Jed.

He hurried toward the door where Erica had stayed

in fear, probably of him more than the corpse. "We have to get out of here."

Her hand still trembling, she gestured toward the body this time.

"He's dead. He's been dead for a while," he reminded her. "We can't help him."

"But we can't just leave him here like that," she said, her voice cracking. "We can't just leave. We need to call the police."

"Someone's already done that for us," he pointed out as the sirens grew louder. And his heart pounded faster with fear and dread.

"If the cops catch us here, I'll be a dead man, too," he said. And he couldn't promise that Erica wouldn't get caught in the crossfire. "There's a shoot-on-sight order out on me."

SHOOT ON SIGHT…

The words echoed in Erica's head. The police would kill Jed rather than try to apprehend him? They considered him that dangerous a criminal?

"Did you touch anything?" he asked, his hand gripping her arm as he pulled her through the reception area toward the front door.

She had left it open behind her, just as she had found it. "I didn't touch anything…"

Because she'd had a bad feeling over all those lights being on at three in the morning. How long had Marcus been dead? Hours? Minutes?

She hadn't checked the body to see if it was as cold as he had told her it was. She glanced back toward Marcus Leighton's office, but it was too far away and Jed's hand too tight around her arm for her to escape him and go back to check now.

Then he ushered her through the front door and into the passenger's side of the van. He turned his head back and forth, his gaze scanning the street before he hurried around to the driver's side. He opened the door and jammed the key in the ignition just as he settled onto the seat. "They're getting close."

Erica glanced back and noticed lights flickering in their rear window. Her neck snapped as Jed pressed hard on the accelerator and swerved around a corner. "You're sure we shouldn't have stayed, that we shouldn't have explained what happened..."

He emitted a bitter chuckle. "I told you—shoot-on-sight. That doesn't give a person any time for explanations."

"But I could—"

"Either get shot with me," he said, as he maneuvered the van around the tight curve of the freeway on-ramp, "or go to jail for aiding and abetting a fugitive."

"Aiding and abetting?" The words chilled Erica's blood, so that she was probably as cold as Marcus Leighton. And of course he would have been cold since his door had been left open, probably when his killer had fled.

"You aided and abetted because you didn't call the police the minute I showed up at your apartment," Jed explained.

With a shudder, she relived that first flash of terror and panic she'd had when she'd realized she had opened her door to Jedidiah Kleyn. "Like you would have let me reach for the phone..."

"It wasn't as if I bound and gagged you," he said. "You had access to your phone. You called your neighbor."

"But you had convinced me of your innocence by

then." And it hadn't even occurred to her to call the police when he had been standing over their daughter's bed, watching her sleep. He had looked like a devoted father, not a dangerous escaped convict.

"You're not so convinced anymore," he said, and the bitter expression on his handsome face turned to one of hurt and disappointment.

Regret clutched at her. "Jed…"

"It's my fault. I shouldn't have brought you along," he said, his voice gruff now with self-condemnation even though she hadn't given him a choice.

But he could have driven off without her when he had gone out the fire escape. His van had been parked in the alley behind her house. Instead, he had waited for her and maybe not just for the lawyer's address. Maybe he had wanted her to be there when Marcus Leighton took back all those things he'd told her that had convinced Erica of Jed's guilt.

A dead man couldn't take back his lies…

"But if I hadn't brought you along," Jed said, "and you heard about his murder, you would have been certain I'd done it." He sighed. "So now you only have suspicions…"

She shook her head, finally pushing aside those initial knee-jerk doubts to make room for common sense. "I know you didn't do it. I was only outside a few minutes before I followed you in, and I didn't hear a shot."

"The gun could have had a silencer," he said, almost as if he wanted to keep her suspicious and fearful of him.

She didn't have any more experience with guns than she did drugs. "Did it?"

"No," he replied. "But I don't think it matters much to you what I say. You can't quite bring yourself to trust me."

"Jed, I spent all these years thinking you were guilty of horrible crimes." The murders had been the worst, but she had felt like a victim, too. She had loved him and believed he'd only used her to provide him with a false alibi.

"You spent all these years thinking that only because Marcus convinced you of my guilt," he said, his voice so gruff with anger that she wondered, if Marcus hadn't already been dead, would Jed have killed him?

She shuddered at the thought. "And now he's dead and we're fleeing the scene of the crime."

He glanced in the rearview mirror. "I don't think the police saw us pulling away. At least they're not following us now."

She turned toward the back window and checked for herself. There were no lights flashing behind them. At this hour, there weren't any other vehicles on the highway. She expelled a breath of relief.

"Or they did see us and noted the plate number and they'll be waiting for us when we go back to your place," he warned her, stealing away her brief moment of relief. "Maybe we should go someplace else until we know for certain."

Erica shuddered again at the thought of armed policemen waiting outside her building or, worse yet, inside her home. "I don't care. I have to go home—to Isobel."

She rarely left her daughter at all and only ever with Mrs. Osborn. If she didn't return, her little girl might feel like Erica had as a child…abandoned and unwanted. Panic clutched at her lungs, stealing away her breath. "I—I have to see my daughter."

Now.

"If they catch us together, you'll lose her," he said.

"You'll go to jail for aiding and abetting me, and she'll go to whoever you appointed her guardian—"

"There's no one…"

She had no idea where her parents were now or even if they were still alive. Until she'd had her daughter, the only real family she'd ever had was Aunt Eleanor. But the elderly woman had died just a few months after Isobel had been born, and she'd left Erica the modest estate in Miller's Valley.

"Then child protective services will take Isobel and place her in a foster home," he said, a muscle twitching in his cheek as he clenched his jaw—as if he battled his own concerns for a daughter he hadn't even known he had.

Erica trembled with nerves, realizing her stubbornness could have cost her little girl the chance at any relationship with her father, as well as the relationship Isobel already had with her mother. Panic gripped her, and she fumbled inside her purse for her cell phone. She should have called the police right away.

Maybe if she called them now, they wouldn't press charges against her. Maybe she wouldn't lose her little girl.

But if she called them and gave up his whereabouts, would they do as Jed had claimed—would they shoot on sight?

SHERIFF GRIFFIN YORK STARED through the bars at him with suspicion hardening eyes that were already shadowed with fatigue. "I don't like that you got a call from your lawyer at this hour," he said as he tested the cell door, as if to make certain that Jefferson James was really locked up.

"Breuker is working hard to represent me," Jefferson replied with satisfaction. Of course, with what he was paying the man, Rick Breuker damn well better be working his ass off. But his attorney might not be the only person Jefferson needed to pay.

Sheriff York wouldn't accept his money, but there were some other officers who weren't as honorable as he was.

"You're not going to get away with all the crimes you committed," York advised him.

He chuckled at the man's naïveté. He'd been surprised and disappointed that a man this young had won the election for sheriff of Blackwoods County. But York wouldn't last in politics, since he had no idea what the real world was like. "You might be surprised…"

James was surprised. His lawyer, Rick Breuker, had called him with the news that the police had been dispatched to Kleyn's lawyer's office. And a dead body had been discovered.

Breuker, who had connections in law enforcement, believed the body belonged to the lawyer, Marcus Leighton. And Kleyn was the number-one suspect, proving wrong the DEA agent's claims of the inmate's innocence, as well as confirming how dangerous Kleyn was to anyone who crossed his path.

That shoot-on-sight order was certain to be carried out now. Kleyn wouldn't be apprehended; he would be dead.

Soon.

Jefferson James had offered an *unofficial* reward for Kleyn's demise to ensure the convict's fate. And once the number-one witness for the prosecution was dead, the case against Jefferson was certain to fall apart. He wouldn't be behind these bars much longer before

York would be opening the door for James, not to take a phone call but to go home.

To his daughter…

Emily had yet to come visit him, but with the reporters hounding her, maybe she just didn't dare leave the house. When Jefferson was freed, he would explain to her that it had all been a horrible misunderstanding. That the only thing he was really guilty of was loving her and wanting to provide for her…

The sheriff studied him through narrowed eyes. "You're up to something…"

Maybe the guy wasn't as naïve as Jefferson had thought. But it wouldn't matter. By the time he figured out the plan, it would be too late for the sheriff to step in and play hero.

Nobody would be able to save Jedidiah Kleyn this time.

THE CONTINGENCY PLAN…

He had intended to destroy the files relating to Kleyn's murder case, just as he had destroyed the lawyer who had ineffectually defended Jedidiah Kleyn so that he had been sentenced to prison for two lifetimes.

Because Marcus Leighton had been so incompetent, he hadn't thought there would actually be anything of value in that file. He hadn't thought that the man had had the balls to hold out on *him*. But Marcus had been keeping a secret, maybe out of guilt or maybe out of misplaced loyalty to Jed.

So he was glad that he'd been thorough, that he'd gone through every paper and scribbled note in the folder before torching it. He had found information in those case files that he could use to finally bring Jedidiah Kleyn to his knees.

War hadn't hurt the man. Neither had prison. But now he knew what would.

Hurting his daughter. Losing her, before he'd ever gotten a chance to spend any time with her, would finally push Jedidiah Kleyn over the edge.

Then, at last, he would prove that the man everyone else had always treated like a superhero was really just a mere mortal.

And mortals died, like Jed would eventually die after he'd finally and sufficiently suffered.

Chapter Six

Betrayal.

It struck him again like a shiv in the chest. And the same woman was betraying him all over again. He closed his hand around hers, snapping her cell phone shut before she could punch in the last *one* of nine-one-one.

"What the hell are you doing?" he demanded. Hadn't she listened to a single warning he'd given her?

"Calling the cops, which is what I should have done the first moment I had the chance," she said, her voice hoarse with self-disgust and fear.

"So much for not doubting me…"

"It doesn't matter what I believe about your guilt or innocence of those murders," she replied. "You were convicted. You were sentenced. And you escaped. You're a fugitive."

"And you're going to turn me over to authorities," he said, bitterness welling up inside him. He never should have started to trust her again.

"I have to," she said, her voice cracking now with emotion and regret. "I can't risk losing Isobel. Not even for you…"

His pulse leapt at the torment apparent in her pale blue eyes. "Not even for me?"

"I should have come forward," she explained, "no matter what your lawyer said. I should have talked to the police then and told them about that night."

"Yes, you should have," he agreed. But now, knowing what she would have told them, he doubted it would have helped. He still would have spent the past three years in prison.

She held tight to her phone and tried to tug free of his grasp. "I need to talk to the police now."

The van swerved slightly as he gripped the wheel with only one hand. But he didn't let go, even though he glanced to the rearview to make sure no one followed them and had noticed the erratic driving. He didn't need to get pulled over now, so close to Miller's Valley and their daughter. "They're not going to believe your story."

His stomach lurched, along with the van across the snow-slick road, when he realized that. He regained control of the vehicle, but that was all he could control of this situation. No matter what she said, it was too late for her to salvage another error in her judgment.

As he had warned her, she would get in trouble for helping him now. Erica would go to jail, and their daughter would go into protective custody with strangers.

Unless...

"Give me the phone," he ordered her in the tone of voice that had always had fellow inmates cowering in fear of him.

Erica didn't cower; she glared at him instead. But she released the phone, tugging her hand free of his, as if unable to bear his touch. She hadn't felt that way that night...

But had she been drugged, as she'd claimed? If she hadn't been drugged, would she have really wanted him at all? She had easily accepted his breaking up with her before he'd left for Afghanistan. She'd never had the feelings for him that he'd had for her—or she never would have doubted his innocence no matter what lies Marcus might have told her.

Because she had no feelings for him but suspicion, he couldn't trust her. Driving with just the one hand on the wheel yet, he punched numbers into her phone.

"Who are you calling?" she asked, her beautiful blue eyes narrowed with suspicion.

Listening to the phone ring, he murmured, "The only lawman I can trust…"

"Agent Cusack," Rowe answered.

"It's me."

"You stubborn son of a…" His future brother-in-law cursed him—obviously not pleased that Jed had terminated their call earlier. "You need to tell me where you are, so I can bring you in. And if you hang up on me again, I will track you down and shoot you myself."

Jed chuckled at the threat. "It's nice to hear your voice, too."

"Your sister can't sleep with worrying over you. She's going crazy." So the DEA agent was more concerned about Macy than Jed.

That was good. Rowe Cusack was the right man for Jed's little sister. The DEA agent loved her like Macy had always deserved to be loved—completely, devotedly and unconditionally. Now if only Jed could find a love like that for himself…

He swallowed a snort of laughter at that thought. Given his luck, there was no way he would ever find a love like his sister had. He'd be lucky to stay alive and alone.

"Tell her not to worry," Jed said. "She'll see me soon."

From the passenger's seat, Erica shot him a glance—obviously wondering about the *she* he talked about and how he expected to see her soon.

Rowe sucked in an audible breath. "You're coming here?"

Jed maneuvered the van onto the slick off-ramp to Miller's Valley. Each mile closer to Isobel brought him farther from Rowe and his sister. "Not yet."

"Damn it, Jed—"

"You will see me soon," he promised, earning another inquisitive glance from Erica. "But you need to get some information for me first."

"I'm already picking up the case files from your lawyer's office tomorrow."

For years Jed had wanted to get his hands on those files, specifically on the ledgers that had provided the motive for killing his business partner. Embezzlement. But he hadn't taken his clients' money. And if he'd been able to go over those ledgers, he might have figured out who had.

"You're too late," Jed informed him. "The files are gone."

Rowe groaned. "Please tell me that you didn't break into his office and take them…"

"I didn't have to break in," Jed replied. "His killer left the door open—"

Rowe cursed now—fervently. "And you walked right into a trap."

"If it was intended as that, I didn't get caught." Or so he hoped; he would find out for certain when they returned to Erica's apartment. "Whoever killed Leighton must have also taken my file from his office."

And just what the hell had Marcus detailed in his file? Erica's address? The fact that she'd been pregnant during the trial?

Leighton had told Jed that he'd never tracked her down, but he hadn't told Jed the truth about anything. Why would he have admitted to knowing her location? He wouldn't have wanted Jed to send someone else to talk to her and learn what Jed had tonight, that Marcus had actually convinced her not to testify.

Despite the heat blowing out of the vents, she wrapped her arms around herself as if she was cold. Or scared.

"This is really bad, Jed," Rowe said, his raspy voice pitched low, probably so that Macy wouldn't overhear him. "You're going to be the number-one suspect for his murder."

He sighed. "I know."

He had been set up. Again.

"Did you...?"

"Hell, no." But he couldn't swear that he wouldn't have killed his lawyer if he had been right about Marcus framing him for murders that his old fraternity brother had actually committed himself.

"I'm sorry, man, that I had to ask and I'm sorry that it happened," Rowe said. "This is a tough break."

"Maybe not," Jed replied. "Although I didn't get to talk to Marcus before he died and find out who paid him to help frame me—"

"What!" The phone cracked with Rowe's exclamation. He'd obviously forgotten to be quiet.

Erica startled as if she'd heard his shout, too.

"Leighton helped set me up," Jed said. His death was proof enough for Jed of his involvement. Marcus's duplicity also explained how Jed had been convicted on just circumstantial evidence and eyewitness testimony that should have been easily discredited. "His partner must have killed him tonight."

Rowe's mind followed the path Jed's had taken. "The killer was worried that Leighton would give him up."

Or *her*.

He glanced at Erica now. Of course she had had no more opportunity to kill Marcus than he had. But another woman could have been involved—Brandon's girlfriend who'd lied in her testimony. Had she been covering up her own guilt? She had really been the last one to see Brandon alive.

She wouldn't have had access to his clients' funds, but Brandon had. He could have embezzled it, and then she killed him to keep the money all to herself. Except for what she'd paid his lawyer.

Then she'd killed him.

Regret tugged at Jed that Marcus was gone now. "He would have told me who'd betrayed me," Jed insisted. He would have either coerced or guilted a confession out of his old friend.

And the killer must have known that, too.

How well did the killer know Marcus? And Jed? Was this about revenge or had he just been a convenient patsy to take the murder rap?

Rowe sighed. "So this is literally a dead end then, man."

"Marcus was paid off."

He never would have been able to afford that historic building if he hadn't been—not with the limited case load he'd had. There hadn't been many files in those drawers, and Jed doubted the killer had taken anyone else's.

"Probably with the money that was embezzled

from my old accounting firm. Track down that money, Rowe."

Jed had wanted to go through those records himself, but Marcus had claimed that he couldn't get permission to bring them in to Blackwoods. Given how corrupt the warden had been, Jed hadn't questioned him. But he should have because Marcus had probably lied about that, too. He just hadn't wanted Jed to track that money down himself because it would have led to Marcus's own wallet.

"During your trial, court-appointed accountants went through those ledgers and bank statements," Rowe said, sharing what he'd learned from the transcripts. "No one was able to figure out where the money had gone. They figured you had secret accounts."

"I didn't." He had never seen any of that money. "But the killer must have. Try to track down the payments that were made to Leighton for throwing my trial."

"What about Erica Towsley?" Rowe asked, seemingly out of the blue. "Who is she?"

Jed chuckled. Rowe had kept interrupting him to keep Jed on the phone long enough to trace the call this time. "Check that angle, too."

"For the money?"

"Follow the money." Jed pulled the van into the alley behind Erica's building.

He doubted it would lead back to her, though. Her vehicle was a piece of junk that looked as if it had more knocks and rattles than a demolition-derby car. And the building where she lived was old, as had been all the furnishings inside her drafty apartment. If she'd been paid off, her payments hadn't been as generous as Leighton's.

"What angle?" Erica whispered.

He shook his head. "And if you can't figure it out, I'll go over the ledgers and statements when I meet up with you."

"If court-appointed accountants couldn't figure it out, I doubt I will be able to," Rowe said.

"Then concentrate on the witnesses," Jed said. "I bet you'll find they were paid off just like Leighton was. Track them down. And I'll track down the money."

"I'll bring the ledgers to you," Rowe offered. "I know where to find you."

Even though the DEA agent couldn't see him, Jed grinned at the man's persistence. "Don't waste your time. I would be gone by the time you got here."

"I could send the police ahead to detain you," Rowe warned him.

"You wouldn't risk it," Jed said with absolute certainty. "You wouldn't risk my life."

Or Macy would probably take Rowe's—no matter how much she loved him. He didn't trust that Erica wouldn't risk his life, though, since she had already almost reported him.

He caught her as she reached for the door handle. "You're not going anywhere."

"Damn it, Jed—"

He clicked off the cell without explaining to Rowe that he hadn't been talking to him.

"Let me go," Erica demanded, her voice rising with panic as she tugged at her arm.

"No. I can't let you go…"

HIS WORDS, SPOKEN SO matter-of-factly, chilled Erica's skin so that goose bumps lifted beneath her heavy clothes.

"I'll scream," she threatened.

"Then I'll have to shut you up." He leaned closer.

Erica closed her eyes, flinching even before he struck her. But he didn't hit her. Instead his gloved fingers slid along her jaw, tipping up her chin. Then his mouth covered hers.

She expected cruelty—for his mouth to punish. But instead his lips slid lightly across hers, brushing gently back and forth. Her breath caught and then escaped in a gasp.

And he deepened the kiss, pressing his mouth tighter against hers until her lips parted. Not for breath.

She didn't need to breathe anymore. She just needed him—needed the passion that warmed her blood and quickened her heart rate. No man had ever affected her like this one.

But those effects hadn't always been good. He had broken her heart when he'd dumped her before his deployment. It hadn't mattered that they'd been broken up, though. She'd spent a year worrying about him and yearning for him.

And loving him.

So it was no wonder she had fallen into his arms and his bed almost literally the minute he had returned home. But he hadn't professed his love then. He had only used her—maybe not for an alibi. But he'd used her all the same.

And broken her heart again.

She lifted her hands between them and pushed against his chest. He had always been muscular, but now his chest was like a concrete wall—hard and immovable. But Erica didn't have to struggle or scream.

He pulled back, his nostrils flaring as he drew in a deep breath.

"I didn't want to do that now," he said.

Finally she breathed, drawing in a sharp breath as his admission stung her pride.

And her heart.

"I wanted to do that the minute you opened the door to me," he continued, "even when I thought you had betrayed me and left me to rot in prison."

"Jed, I didn't—"

"I realize now that you didn't betray me three years ago, but you were about to do it now," he reminded her. "You can't call the police, Erica."

"I can't," she agreed, "because you took my phone." But even if he hadn't, she doubted she would have been able to punch in that last digit. She was almost grateful that he had taken the phone from her.

Who had he called to help him? Who was the lawman he trusted? A guard from the prison? It had sounded like they were all corrupt. Or the DEA agent whose badge he had used to trick her into opening the door for him?

"You have a landline in your apartment," he said. "So you're not going inside without me."

"But if Mrs. Osborn sees you, she will call the police for certain." Taking the impossible decision out of Erica's hands but putting custody of her daughter and Erica's own freedom at risk.

Jed shrugged off her concern. "I doubt she'll recognize me. I don't look like the photo they keep showing of me on the news."

No. He looked even more dangerous than the mug shot taken before his trial. After three years in Blackwoods Penitentiary, he was undoubtedly more dangerous.

"I'm not worried about *her* calling the police on me." He narrowed his eyes, which were dark with suspicion as he stared at her.

He was worried about Erica. Even though she had explained why she hadn't come forward at his trial, he didn't trust her, and now that he was dead, Marcus Leighton couldn't confirm that he was the reason she hadn't provided Jed with an alibi. In addition to that, she had almost reported him to authorities, so she couldn't blame him for not trusting her.

"I won't call the police," she promised. "I'm not sure I believe you completely about that shoot-on-sight order. But I can't risk it."

His gaze widened slightly, but then he shook his head. "Somehow I don't think I'm the one you're worried about losing."

She had already lost him twice. First to Afghanistan and then to prison. But then, he had never really been hers to lose.

"I can't risk Isobel's safety," she said as she pushed open the passenger door.

He didn't stop her this time, and she felt a moment's flash of disappointment as she stepped onto the snow-covered pavement.

"I can't risk her getting shot in the crossfire," she said. "That's why you need to get into whatever vehicle you brought here—" she gestured at a car and a van parked in the alley "—and drive as far away from us as you can get."

"You're right," he agreed—almost too easily as he slammed shut the driver's door after joining her in the alley. "I never would have come to you if I hadn't thought you alibi-ing me would be the fastest way to get my conviction overturned."

"I'm sorry..."

"And I never should have let you come with me to

see Leighton," he said, his voice gruff with guilt and frustration.

"I didn't give you a choice," she reminded him as she headed toward the back door of her building. "I didn't tell you his address."

"But I could have gotten it out of you…"

He could have—had he kissed her like he just had. So she didn't argue with him, just closed her eyes and relived those few brief moments when his lips had covered hers.

"I'm not giving you a choice now," he said as he slid his arm around her.

She opened her eyes, both anticipating and fearing another kiss. But he wasn't even looking at her.

He had only reached around her for the door knob. "I'm going up to your apartment with you," he said. "I'm going to make sure you and Isobel are safe before I leave."

She shook her head. "Mrs. Osborn—"

"Will never get a good look at my face," he said as he opened the door. "No one has recognized me since the prison break. No one will."

The collar was up on his dark-colored wool coat, but it didn't hide much of his face. Dark stubble did that, as did his expression, which was so intimidating that nobody was likely to stare at him long enough to recognize him.

Erica drew in a shaky breath and inhaled the scent that had always been Jed's alone—rain fresh but musky male. "You'll leave once you see Isobel?"

He nodded.

"Okay." She followed him inside and up the back stairs to her apartment. "Let me go in first and distract Mrs. Osborn."

Jed was already reaching for her door, too, but he didn't have to turn the knob. It stood ajar, the apartment so dark inside that only shadows spilled out into the dimly lit hallway. Something clattered to the hardwood floor inside, and Jed shoved open the door and bolted into the living room.

"Stop," she called after him in a loud whisper. When she was watching Isobel, Mrs. Osborn usually left the doors open between her apartment and Erica's. And the older woman often dropped things.

But Jed didn't stop.

So Erica rushed inside after him. He wasn't alone. But it wasn't Mrs. Osborn he grappled with in the dark living room. The black-clothed figure was nearly as big as he was. But not big enough to overpower Jed, even though the man swung a punch at him. While it connected, it didn't even faze Jed.

Then Jed swung back, knocking the man to the ground. He reached for the intruder and dragged him to his feet, but the man broke free of Jed's grasp.

He turned toward the open door. Erica stood there, blocking the exit. Her heart slammed against her ribs, and her muscles froze so that she couldn't move out of the way.

But he didn't charge at her. He didn't even look at her. He kept his head down, as Jed had demonstrated he did so that he wasn't recognized. Then the man turned again and ran down the hall toward Isobel's room.

Despite his size, Jed's reflexes were quick and his stride fast as he pursued the intruder. Erica's muscles recovered as fear and determination pulsed through her, and she chased after them.

Her primary concern was protecting her daughter.

She wouldn't let anyone hurt her little girl. Size and muscle was no match for a mother's protective instinct.

Jed's primary concern was obviously catching the intruder, since he didn't spare so much as a glance toward the little twin bed as they ran past it. The men did not even stop inside the small bedroom. The intruder vaulted through the open window, and, with a hard thump on the metal, Jed followed him out onto the fire escape.

The curtains fluttered in the breeze blowing through the open window, whipping the hot-pink satin against the walls. It was freezing in the room, but it wasn't nearly as cold as the blood pumping hard and fast with fear through Erica's veins.

She stopped next to her daughter's bed, but she didn't even need to look down at the tangled blankets to know that it was empty.

Her baby was gone.

Chapter Seven

"It'll be too late. By the time you get there, he'll be well on his way somewhere else," Macy warned her husband-to-be.

Rowe cursed and dropped his car keys back onto the desk before dropping his body onto the chair behind his desk. "I know. But…"

"But what?" she asked. "You've been keeping something from me, and we promised we'd never do that."

"I want to protect you," he said.

"But I'm not in danger."

"Not anymore," he agreed, his deep voice vibrating with the torment of remorse for what she had recently endured. He blamed himself.

She blamed Warden Jefferson James.

"But Jed is," she said.

"Macy…" The torment hadn't left his voice.

Her pulse quickened. "How much danger?" she demanded to know.

"You know everyone considers him a cop killer…"

"That's why you went on the news," she said, suddenly realizing. "You wanted to put doubts in the minds of the officers looking for him. You wanted to make it so that they won't shoot first and ask questions later."

A muscle twitched along his tightly clenched jaw, and

he nodded. "Someone put out a shoot-on-sight order on him."

"Someone?" She snorted. "It's Warden James. He doesn't want Jed able to testify against him." And the unscrupulous man had already proven he had no problem with killing. Of course, he always had preferred that others get the blood on their hands instead of him getting it on his.

Rowe nodded again, sending a lock of blond hair over his furrowed brow. "Someone even put out an unofficial reward…"

"For my brother's murder?" She sucked in a breath as pain jabbed her heart. "Does he know this?"

"I warned him about the shoot-on-sight order. I didn't know about the reward until another officer told me what he'd heard."

"So Jed knows he's in danger out there, but he won't come in?"

Rowe shook his head. "I promised I'd protect him."

Her brother had always been stubborn…but she understood what he was thinking. "He won't turn himself in until he proves his innocence."

"His lawyer was murdered—"

"Marcus?" She wouldn't have chosen the man to represent her brother for a parking ticket, much less murder. But Jed had always been loyal to his friends. She suspected they couldn't say the same.

"It looks like he was paid off to throw the trial," Rowe said. "I was already beginning to think that from going over the court transcripts."

Macy had been premed, not prelaw, but she'd thought so, too. "He never objected to anything."

"And he didn't really challenge the eyewitness testimony," Rowe said. "Your brother asked me to find the witnesses."

She met her fiancé's gaze. "Jed didn't kill his lawyer."

"I had to ask him..." He groaned. "If someone had helped set me up to spend the rest of my life in a hell-hole like Blackwoods..."

"I know." She crossed the room and dropped onto his lap, looping her arm around his neck. "I understand why you would have doubted him. But he's not a killer. He won't hurt the witnesses."

Rowe pressed a kiss to her lips, the stubble on his jaw erotically scraping her skin. "You even wondered if he might not want revenge more than justice."

"We have to make sure that we help him choose justice. Find the witnesses."

Rowe sighed. "I'd rather find Jed. Bringing him in is the only way to make sure he stays safe."

He wouldn't be safe in custody, either. They both knew it. "The only way to make sure my brother stays safe is to prove his innocence."

"We have to find the real killer," Rowe agreed.

Before Jed found him...

THE FIRE ESCAPE VIBRATED beneath Jed's feet as he chased the dark shadow down into the alley he had left just moments ago with Erica. His borrowed van was parked alongside hers. If he had done as she'd asked and gotten into it and left...

She would have walked into her apartment alone—and at the mercy of a brute of a man who'd immediately attacked Jed. If the guy had attacked Erica...

His fist stung from the one blow he'd connected, which had knocked the guy back on his feet and loose from his grasp. Jed hadn't been able to catch him since.

The guy had been just enough faster than he was that Jed hadn't been able to outrun him in the hall. And he'd lost him on the fire escape.

He dropped off the last rung of the metal ladder and connected with the asphalt, his ankles stinging at the impact. Jed focused on the snowfall, trying to discern footprints. But the wind had whipped up, swirling around the light dusting of snow, so that he couldn't track him. But the guy had to be around here somewhere. The short hairs lifting on his nape, Jed could feel him close. Maybe crouched behind one of the vans?

Jed moved silently, as he had learned to move during his deployment. He crept closer to the van and peered through the windows, trying to spy a shadow on the other side. Then he held still—perfectly still—and waited. As he'd learned in his National Guard training, he could hold his breath and slow his heart rate.

Could the man he'd chased from Erica's apartment do the same? Eventually the guy would have to breathe, and Jed would hear him as he listened intently.

But he didn't hear a breath. He heard a scream. Erica's scream. It rent the eerie, predawn silence.

His heart lurched, shifting in his chest. "God, no…"

Instead of wasting time to go back through the building, Jed jumped for the last rung of the fire escape and pulled himself up. As he vaulted up the steps, his heart pounded hard with fear and dread.

Had he followed out a staged distraction while the guy's accomplice had stayed behind for Erica and Isobel? Had that accomplice already hurt them?

He stopped outside the window and peered into the room to assess the situation before rushing in blind. Erica stood alone by Isobel's bed, her hands clasped against her mouth as if she fought to hold back more screams. He scanned the corners of the room, checking for a man holding a gun on her. Because if this was an ambush, it would be for him. And Jed wouldn't be able to protect her and their daughter if he was dead.

But seeing Erica in such fear and pain was killing him. He stepped through the window and joined her inside the room. "You screamed—"

She whirled toward him. "She's gone! He took her, Jed! He took our daughter!"

He cupped her shoulders and then her face in his slightly shaking palms. "No. He wasn't carrying anything down the fire escape. He didn't take her."

He damn well wouldn't have let the bastard grab their child. If he had seen the man even reach toward the bed, he would have finally become that murderer everyone already thought he was.

Erica's voice cracked with hysteria. "She's gone..."

He pulled her into his arms, clutching her trembling body close to his chest. "He didn't take her..."

But Jed must have been right about the accomplice. Instead of staying behind, though, he had gone ahead—with Isobel. And the other man had provided the distraction so that he could get away with the child.

Jed had only known about Isobel for a few hours, but he'd already lost her. He clutched Erica closer, but instead of offering comfort, he was seeking it. He didn't deserve it, though; this was his fault.

Isobel had been taken because of him. Whoever had framed him for murder had found an even more effective way to hurt him than sending him to prison.

NO MATTER HOW CLOSE Jed held her, Erica felt no comfort. His heart raced at the same frantic pace as hers. He was scared, too. Maybe even more scared than she was because he had seen more horrors in his life than she had in her relatively sheltered one.

Even though she watched the news, those things happened to other people—not her. In her safe little world here in Miller's Valley, her child could never be taken. Her child would not be harmed. But Jed had shaken her safe world. He'd brought danger and murder to her life, making all horrible things possible. Even to her sweet angel baby...

Sobs broke free of her control, shaking her—making her so sick with fear that she nearly gagged. Big hands patted her back, trying again to offer comfort. But his touch chilled her, making her shudder.

"Erica, we'll find her," he promised. "We'll get her back."

"No, I want you out of here!" she yelled, wedging her hands between them so that she could shove him away from her—out of her safe, little world. "I want you to leave! This is your fault. This is all your fault!"

He flinched. He was so big and muscular that he probably couldn't be physically hurt. But she had emotionally hurt him. Even though he had only just discovered he had a daughter, he cared about Isobel. He was as scared as she was.

A twinge of guilt penetrated her fear and hysteria. But anger pushed that guilt away. "It's your fault that my baby is gone!"

Jed's breath caught, and his eyes widened.

But she didn't care anymore that he was hurting, too. She stepped back again. She didn't care if he got hurt, either. She was going to call the police this time. She couldn't waste another moment worrying about Jedidiah Kleyn.

But before she could turn away from him, a small hand slipped into hers and tugged on her fingers.

"Mommy, I'm not gone," a soft voice informed her. "I'm right here."

Erica whirled around and dropped to her knees to wrap up Isobel in her arms. "Oh, sweetheart…" Tears streaked down her face.

"Mommy, why are you crying?"

She couldn't tell the child about the man who had broken into their home. But she couldn't lie to her, either. "I was scared, honey, when I found your bed empty."

"I was at Mrs. Osborn's," the little girl explained. "I woked up and she tooked me over there."

Erica glanced up, her nerves returning as she discovered her neighbor standing in the bedroom doorway. The older woman's gaze was focused on Jed's face, her faded blue eyes narrowed with suspicion.

"Mrs. Osborn—" Erica jumped up and headed toward her, trying to block her view of Jed. But he was so much taller than she was—until he crouched down in front of their daughter.

"What's going on here?" Mrs. Osborn demanded to know with equal parts anger and fear.

With a pointed glance at Isobel to indicate that she didn't want to talk in front of the child, Erica guided the woman back down the hall toward the front door. "Nothing's wrong…"

Not now that her baby was back.

"I heard screaming and nearly called the authorities." Mrs. Osborn stared down the hall toward the dark shadow enveloping the little girl. "Looks like I should have called."

"No. I just overreacted to finding Isobel's bed

empty," Erica explained with a self-deprecating chuckle. "It's late and I'm tired."

"And you're not alone," Mrs. Osborn said. "Who is that man? I've never seen him around before..."

She had never seen any man around Erica unless he was a client of her accounting business. After Jed, she hadn't dared trust another man—especially when she had Isobel's safety to worry about even more than her own.

Her stomach pitched again with the horror over what could have happened to her baby had Isobel been in the apartment when that man had broken in...

The old woman's wrinkled brow furrowed into deeper lines of confusion. "Actually I think that I might have seen him before..."

"He's an old friend of mine," Erica said. "You've probably seen him in some pictures I've had around here." She opened the door to the hall before the woman could ask to see those photos.

But Mrs. Osborn was already peering into the living room and, with a trembling hand gesturing toward it, noted a lamp lying on the floor.

Erica forced a smile. "He—he couldn't find the lights in the dark."

Mrs. Osborn leaned closer and clasped her hand. "If he's threatening you, I'll go back to my apartment and call the police. I'll get you help."

"I don't need help," Erica lied.

She desperately needed help. She had stumbled into a murder scene, had had her apartment broken into and, for long, horrific moments, had believed that her daughter had been abducted.

"Everything's fine." She glanced back at Jed and forced a smile. "He really is a friend."

"Oh." Mrs. Osborn nodded in sudden understanding. "He's an old *boy*friend."

"Yes." She hadn't had to lie this time.

For a short while before his deployment, Jed had been her boyfriend. Their connection had been so instant and deep that she had believed it could have lasted forever.

But, like everyone else who had mattered in her life, he hadn't given her the chance.

Now she couldn't give him one. She had to get rid of him this time—had to make sure that he took his danger out of her previously safe world.

She clasped Mrs. Osborn's hand tighter—ready to give her the message the older woman had already suspected Erica wanted to give her.

Call the police...

JEDIDIAH KLEYN HAD CHANGED. That was the first thing he'd noticed before he'd punched the man. With his buzz cut and bulky muscles, Jed didn't look all that physically different from the war hero who had returned from his tour in Afghanistan with a Purple Heart.

But he was very different—mentally and emotionally.

He was harder. Tougher. Ruthless in a way that he had never been. Jed would undoubtedly kill to protect the woman and her child.

Before Jed and Erica had walked in on him, he'd had time to look at all the *family* photos inside the apartment. But the kid hadn't been in her bed. Not that Jed would have given him time to grab the little girl. He had been too focused on catching him.

And killing him?

He rubbed his jaw, which had swollen from the blow Jed had dealt him. He snorted in derision at his quick flash of anger. He had no right to be mad about it. He'd had that one coming. Hell, he had a lot more than one coming to him.

But Jed wouldn't land another punch. Jed had already won too much in his life.

It was *his* turn to win.

And Jedidiah Kleyn's turn to die.

Chapter Eight

Trying not to imagine who she had entertained here, Jed ignored the red walls and white lace curtains of Erica's bedroom. His attention was focused on the tiny female tucked under the red-and-white quilt. She slept deeply. Peacefully. He would probably never sleep again.

But then it was already morning. Sunshine radiated through those lace curtains, warming the hardwood floor and enveloping the bed and the sleeping child in a circle of ethereal light.

Voices emanated from the living room. The old woman had left a while ago. Who the hell...

He spared one last glance at his sleeping daughter, assuring himself that she was safe in Erica's room. There was no fire escape so that someone could break the window and quickly grab her without being noticed. Isobel was much safer in her mother's room.

But what about her mother?

He didn't hear her voice. As he crept down the hall toward the living room, he realized the voices came from the television set. Erica stood before it, the remote clasped in her slightly trembling hand.

"Isn't that too loud?" he asked, then remembered that their daughter was a sound sleeper.

Erica didn't bother reminding him. She just gestured at the screen. "They're running your story again."

He didn't even glance at the TV. "That's not *my* story."

Someone else had concocted the story that had sent him to prison for crimes he hadn't committed.

"The part about breaking out of prison and being an escaped convict is your story," she said. "And that's what Mrs. Osborn will see when she watches this. She'll recognize you. You have to leave before she calls the police."

She tossed the remote onto the couch and moved toward the door, as if to see him out. But he didn't follow her. Instead he headed to where he'd brawled with the intruder. She had righted the lamp that had fallen to the floor, but the shade was dented from where it had struck the hardwood.

He would have had Rowe check it for prints, but the man had worn gloves. What had he been looking for? The lamp sat atop a bureau crowded with picture frames. Isobel's face, so much like his sister Macy's, smiled out of most of them from infancy to her current age. The drawers were shut, no papers disturbed.

Jed doubted the man had been looking for files like those taken from Marcus Leighton's office. Jed was afraid that what he'd been looking for had been across the hall with Mrs. Osborn...

"I'm sure your neighbor is asleep in her bed after her late night," Jed assured her. The woman was very old, her eyes foggy as if she had cataracts. He doubted she had been able to see much more than his shadowy outline, let alone enough of his features to recognize his face.

Instead of worrying about her neighbor, Erica should

be in her bed with their daughter. Dark circles rimmed her pale blue eyes. But she trembled with anxiety.

"You need to leave," she insisted. "Now. Before it's too late."

"You really think I should leave?" he asked. "After what happened last night?"

Her breath shuddered out as her mind followed a different path into the past. "A man died."

"I didn't kill Marcus." He'd thought he had convinced her of that, but obviously she still had her doubts about him.

"I know." She pointed toward the TV again. "But the authorities won't. They'll think you're even more dangerous than they already do."

They were already going to shoot him on sight; now maybe they wouldn't even wait to make sure it was him before they started firing. Would sticking close to Erica and Isobel keep them safe or put them in more danger?

"If I leave, that man might come back," he warned her.

"And if you stay, and Mrs. Osborn recognizes you, he won't be the only one breaking into my home." She glanced toward her door, her eyes widening as if she could imagine a battering ram breaking apart the wood and a SWAT team bursting into her living room.

He could imagine the same thing, but he could also imagine that man coming back…for her and Isobel. And his gut told him that man would prove much more dangerous than any lawman with a shoot-on-sight order. "I can't just leave you…"

"Why not?" she asked. "You didn't come here to protect me. You came here to force me to provide you with an alibi and clear your name. I can't do that. I can't perjure myself and swear that you never left me that night."

"I didn't want you to perjure yourself," he said. "I wanted you to tell the truth."

"I have," she said.

He wished he could be certain that she told the truth. But after learning that yet another friend had betrayed him, he dared not trust a woman he really hadn't known very well at all. She hadn't just kept his possible alibi from the police; she'd kept his daughter from him, too.

"So why are you still here?" Erica asked with such intensity that the question must have been nagging at her for a while.

He gestured toward her bedroom, to where their daughter lay sleeping. He couldn't put into words what he already felt for his child—the protectiveness, the affection, the devotion...

"Until a few hours ago, you didn't even know Isobel existed," Erica reminded him.

"Whose fault was that?" he asked, the question slipping out with his bitterness. She could have gone to his trial or visited him in prison to at least let him know that he had become a father.

Her delicately featured face flushed, but she shook her head in rejection of any culpability. "It was Marcus Leighton's fault for convincing me of your guilt. If there was any chance that you were the killer your own lawyer thought you were, I didn't want you to have anything to do with my baby."

Jed couldn't fault her for that. She was a good mother. Instead he cursed the man whom he'd once considered a friend.

Macy had wanted to get him a better lawyer, one with more experience with criminal cases, but he had been loyal. Why hadn't Marcus? The man had promised that no one else would work as hard at proving Jed's innocence than he would, and Jed had trusted him.

Now he knew better than to ever trust again.

"Go," Erica urged him. "Find out who bribed him to betray you. Find out who wanted you to spend the rest of your life in prison."

"I intend to," he said. That hadn't changed, but it was no longer his first priority. "Proving my innocence was my whole reason for leaving during the riot at Blackwoods."

"So go," she urged him again—almost desperately. She had been afraid of him earlier—when he'd tricked her into opening the door. But this fear, haunting her blue eyes, was even greater. She wasn't afraid of him anymore, but she was afraid of the danger he'd brought into her life.

"I can't leave without you and Isobel," he said. Chances were good her intruder would return. Soon.

She shook her head. "We can't go with you. We can't live on the run. You can't ask that of us…"

"I don't want you living on the run," he said. "I just want you living. I want you safe."

But he wanted more than that. He wanted *her* in every way. He stepped closer to her, and she must have seen desire in his eyes because her breath audibly caught.

And maybe she wanted him, too, because she leaned toward him. He lowered his head to hers. She gasped at his nearness, and her breath warmed his lips. Then he covered her mouth with his.

A man on the run from authorities and a killer, he had no time for kisses. But, in this moment, there was nothing he would rather be doing than kissing Erica Towsley.

ERICA LIFTED HER HANDS, pressing her palms against his chest. She needed to push him away—to push him out of the door and out of her and Isobel's lives.

But instead, her fingers curled into his shirt, and she clutched him closer. Rising up on tiptoe, she pressed her mouth tighter to his. He parted her lips, deepening the kiss.

His tongue touched hers and ignited a fire within her. Her legs trembled as desire rushed through her. Her nipples tightened, and heat filled her stomach. And all those disjointed memories from that night—the night they conceived their daughter—flitted through her mind.

As if he felt her trembling, he swung her up in his arms—clasping her tight to his chest. And he kissed her more deeply, his tongue sliding in and out of her mouth until she moaned.

She ran her hands up the back of his neck to clasp his head, and his closely cropped hair tickled her palms. She tingled all over as passion pulsed inside her.

He groaned and moved, carrying her over to the couch. He lowered her to the cushions and followed her down, covering her body with his.

He was so big. So muscular. So heavy, even though he balanced most of his weight on his bulging arms. She wrapped her arms around him and pulled him closer. Then she wrapped her legs around his waist and arched into him—wanting, *needing,* more.

He lifted his mouth from hers and stared into her eyes; his were dark and hot with desire. "Erica…?"

How could she have ever thought that he had drugged and taken her choice away from her? Even though he'd been locked up for three years, he was giving her a choice now—instead of just taking what she was freely willing to give.

Why was she so willing? Maybe she had been locked up, too, for the past few years—afraid to trust because of what she had considered such a betrayal of her love. But Jed hadn't betrayed her.

If anyone had betrayed anyone, she had betrayed him when she had let Marcus Leighton make her doubt him. She'd already apologized, but she had to say it again. "I'm sorry…"

With a shudder, he rose up—pulling away as if she'd rejected him. "No, I'm sorry," he said. "This is crazy. We can't do this—"

"We shouldn't," she said.

For so many reasons. The most pressing was that he couldn't stay. He was a man on the run who had already brought her nothing but heartbreak and danger.

"But we can," she continued. It wouldn't make up to him the three years of his life that he'd lost, but it might help them regain some of the closeness and promise they'd had before he had gone off to Afghanistan and broken off their relationship.

"And I want to." She grasped his shirt in both fists and tugged him down toward her.

His hands covered hers, and he stared at her, his gaze dark with a breath-stealing intensity. Then he pulled her fingers from his shirt.

At least one of them had the sense to realize this was neither the time nor the place for making love. But still she had to blink back tears of disappointment. Then she was blinking to clear her eyes as he pulled off his shirt and tossed it onto the floor next to the couch. All rippling, sinewy muscle, he was so damn sexy.

Her breath caught as desire overwhelmed her. She

touched him, sliding her fingertips across the hair-dusted silky skin. Then she lifted up to press her lips to his chest. His heart thudded against her mouth.

"Erica..."

He lowered his head and kissed her—deeply. And she kissed him back with all the passion she felt for him. It pulsed low in her body, winding a pressure tight inside her. It filled her ears with the sound of her own blood rushing through her veins.

But a rapid beep, beep, beep broke the grip of desire, clearing her head, so that she heard the broadcast announcement:

"Early this morning the governor has issued a special press release. In order to apprehend the convicts who escaped during the prison riot at Blackwoods Penitentiary in northern Michigan, he has put a bounty on the head of each of the prisoners. These bounties will be paid either to the person who actually apprehends these escapees or to the person who provides information leading to their apprehension."

His voice quavering with excitement, the reporter stated the amount on each convict. "But the highest bounty will be paid for the apprehension of cop killer Jedidiah Kleyn."

A pithy curse escaped Jed's lips with a hiss of breath. "That's not a bounty," he murmured. "It's a death warrant..."

He hadn't been lying about the shoot-on-sight order. In light of the bounty, he'd probably actually down-played how much danger he was really in.

"You have to leave," she urged him as panic gripped her.

Mrs. Osborn might have believed that Jed was Erica's friend, but that wouldn't matter if she recognized his photo and thought she could collect that kind of money for reporting his location.

And she would recognize the photo that filled the television screen. It wasn't his mug shot, with his full head of dark hair and clean-shaven square jaw, that they had previously shown. This was his prison ID that must have finally been retrieved from the ruins that was all that was left of Blackwoods Penitentiary. In this picture, there was more stubble on his jaw than his shaved head. And he looked hard and dangerous—like he did now.

He swore again. Then he grabbed up his shirt from the floor and dragged it over his head. "Erica—"

"Go," she said, the panic stealing away her breath as it pressed heavily on her lungs. "You have to get out of here before it's too late."

But then a noise penetrated the thin window panes of her home. Sirens.

It was already too late.

The authorities were coming for him with orders to shoot on sight.

"YOU MANIPULATIVE MONSTER," Drake Ketchum shouted through the bars of the Blackwoods County jail.

A smile tugged at Jefferson's lips. "Are you supposed to be talking to me without my lawyer present?" he goaded the ambitious, young Blackwoods County district attorney.

"I'm going to trace this back to you and add it to the other charges you're going down for," Ketchum threatened.

"Trace what back to me?"

"You're behind the bounty," Ketchum said. "You talked the governor into it!"

Jefferson chuckled. "You give me entirely too much

credit. Do you really think I'd still be in here if the governor was taking my calls?"

Ketchum was the real master of manipulation; at the arraignment, he'd talked the judge into denying bail for Jefferson.

"Then you put your sleazy attorney up to it."

Jefferson shrugged. "Prove it," he challenged the man. "You won't be able to do that any easier than you'll be able to prove I ordered the murder of an undercover DEA agent, since your star witness is dead."

Sheriff York stood beside Ketchum—two young men who were stupid and idealistic enough to believe they ruled this county. Jefferson nearly laughed again, but it was York who chuckled this time.

"Kleyn isn't dead," the sheriff said.

He shrugged again—unconcerned because they were entirely too concerned. "You have him in protective custody then?"

"Not yet," York admitted.

"Then you better get him there soon," he spoke to Ketchum, "or you're going to lose that star witness for sure—what with every law-enforcement officer and bounty hunter in this state and probably most of the surrounding ones gunning for him."

Ketchum's gaze slid from his to the sheriff. "He's right. You better find him first."

Jefferson was enjoying this visit immensely. It was good for these young fools to know who really had all the power. "And, since you don't know where he is, I feel compelled to point out that you don't know for certain if he's still alive."

"Thanks to that bounty we know," Ketchum replied. "If he was dead, someone would have tried to claim it."

Jefferson nodded. "True. Unless the person Kleyn's

in the most danger from has no use for the bounty. If that convict is actually as innocent as he claims and the DEA agent believes he is, then there's someone who wants him dead even more…"

"Than you do?"

He chuckled at Ketchum's weak attempt to trap him. "You're going to have to do better than that," he warned the man. Then he turned to the sheriff. "And so are you if you want to bring that escapee back alive."

"You should have figured out by now that the man isn't easy to kill," York reminded him. "Your fellow guards have already told us that you ordered his murder after the prison doctor's. But then the riot broke out."

And everything had gone to hell. Because of Jedidiah Kleyn. Now it was his turn to go to hell.

Chapter Nine

In tight fists, Jed gripped the steering wheel of Erica's van. He had to stay in control. For so many reasons...

The most important one slept in her car seat in the back. He glanced into the rearview mirror at the reflection of her peaceful face. Since he'd met her, he had spent a lot of time watching Isobel sleep.

Then he turned toward the woman who sat in the passenger seat beside him. She had not slept at all the previous night, and from the tension gripping her body and beautiful face, she would not sleep anytime soon.

She was another reason for him to stay in control. The other was the authorities they had barely escaped, passing the patrol cars minutes before they would have pulled up to her building.

He had to stay calm and keep his wits about him because not only would the police be after him now, but so would every bounty hunter and civilian who wanted to collect the reward for his head.

Just being with him was putting Erica and Isobel in danger, too. He drew in a deep breath, bracing himself for the answer to the question he had to ask her. "Why did you agree to leave with me?"

Erica turned toward the backseat and their sleeping daughter. "Mrs. Osborn will tell the police that I called you a friend. Then they'll believe that I'm aiding and abetting you. They would arrest me and take Isobel off to child protective services—just like you warned me."

"I'm sorry..." That he had been right, and he was also sorry for letting her go along with him to confront Marcus. The minute he'd realized she had been duped just like the jury of his peers, he should have left her and Isobel. But he hadn't entirely believed that she was telling the truth. He couldn't trust her.

He shouldn't trust anyone. But to protect her and their daughter, he had no choice.

"Now we're forced to live like you—" her voice cracked on a sob, but she forced it down with a deep breath "—on the run."

"I'm sorry..." He glanced into the rearview mirror again but not to watch their daughter sleep. Instead he tracked the vehicle that was closing the careful distance at which the driver had been following them from Miller's Valley.

He'd taken her van and had left his in the alley because authorities had probably figured out by now that the guard's van was missing. They would have issued an APB on that license plate. But maybe one had already been issued on Erica's, too.

Living on the run might be the least of her concerns because it looked as though they were about to get caught. The only question was, who was doing the catching...

ERICA'S BACK PRESSED AGAINST the seat as the van accelerated. She followed Jed's gaze to the rearview mirror. "Is someone following us?"

"I think so," he tersely admitted.

"Is it a police officer?" She turned around to check again for flashing lights.

He shook his head. "It's not a patrol car, and it doesn't look like an unmarked police car, either."

"You think it's him—the intruder," she said, as he accelerated some more.

"It could be a bounty hunter." His mouth curved into a cynical half smile, as he added, "Hell, it could even be your neighbor Mrs. Osborn determined to collect that reward."

An image of the old woman chasing them down with her battered Bonneville elicited a giggle from Erica. "The doctor took away her license until she gets her cataracts removed."

"So it's not Mrs. Osborn," he surmised, his half smile slipping into a full grin for just a minute before it disappeared.

"No, it's not."

How much had he had to grin about over the past three years? Nothing, she would bet.

"It might not be anyone," he said. "It could just be someone who's coincidentally traveling the same road we are."

"Toward your friend's house?"

When they had heard the sirens in the distance, he had urged her to come with him. He promised that he knew someone, probably the one lawman he had faith in, who would be able to protect her and Isobel. And in the heat and panic of the moment, she had believed her instincts were right and trusted him.

She hoped like hell she wouldn't regret giving that trust because it wasn't just her heart at risk this time—it was her daughter's life.

Jed shrugged, but his nonchalant gesture didn't fool her since he focused on the mirror again.

"You don't think it's a coincidence," she said. "And if it is that person who broke into my house, then he's going to know where you're bringing us."

"I'll lose him." And he accelerated again. But her van was old, and the engine shuddered instead of shifting. He cursed beneath his breath.

"You're not going to lose him in this." The mechanic had warned her that she needed a new transmission. However, she didn't often have to drive anywhere in Miller's Valley, so she had been waiting until she needed to travel somewhere. She hadn't imagined that the van would have to make two long-distance trips within a few hours.

And that it would have to outrun a faster vehicle. The rev of a powerful engine echoed as the car behind them accelerated.

They should have taken his vehicle, but he'd explained that the police might have already been looking for it. Now she wished they'd taken their chances with the police...

She repeated the fear that was causing that fluttery panic in her chest again. "He's going to follow to wherever you're bringing us."

She really should have asked where he was bringing them; she shouldn't have given her trust so blindly. But after how she'd given him her mistrust in the past, she'd felt as if she'd owed him.

But she couldn't worry about Jed anymore; she had to worry about her daughter. "Isobel will still be in danger."

"Not with Rowe Cusack."

"The DEA agent?" she asked. The one whose badge Jed had flashed to fool her. "He's been helping you?"

A muscle twitched along his jaw as he glanced into the rearview mirror. And he didn't reply.

"Jed?" she prodded him, her stomach clenching with apprehension. "Does he know you're coming? Is he *really* helping you?"

"He will."

But the DEA agent wouldn't be able to help them if they couldn't get to him. The car had gained on them, coming up so fast and close that it struck the rear bumper of the van.

Isobel woke up with a scream that echoed Erica's.

Erica fought back her own panic and forced a smile as she leaned over her seat to face her daughter. "It's okay, sweetheart. No reason to be afraid."

The car connected with their rear bumper again. Even though she saw it coming, a scream bubbled back up in Erica's throat. She choked it down and offered Isobel another shaky smile. "See, it's just like playing bumper cars at the fair."

Isobel's eyes widened. "But this isn't a bumpa car, Mommy."

"We're just pretending it is," Erica explained. But the other car wasn't just pretending; it really was hitting them, and very hard.

The tires skidded as they tried to grip the snow-covered pavement. She needed new tires, too. But that was another thing she had thought she would be able to put off purchasing for a while. The van spun around, nearly sliding off the road into one of the ditches on the side. Because the ditches were so deep and usually filled with water, people drowned if their vehicles went off into them.

Isobel screamed, but with no fear this time. She had bought Erica's story of make-believe. So when the car struck them again, the little girl squealed with excitement and joy.

Erica blinked against the sting of tears and hung onto her fake smile even as she turned toward Jed. He wasn't smiling. He was so focused on driving that he might not have even heard the lie that she had told their daughter. He'd heard the story she'd given Mrs. Osborn, too—first about her emergency in Grand Rapids and then about Jed being her friend. He probably thought she lied very easily and very often. He would never trust her now, and she didn't blame him.

His knuckles turned from dark red to white as he gripped the steering wheel. And a muscle twitched in his cheek, above his rigidly held jaw. He was determined to protect them. But it was obvious that he wasn't convinced that he could.

Neither was Erica.

A CRASH REVERBERATED inside Macy's head, jerking her awake. Her neck ached from how she'd fallen asleep leaning over the armrest of a chair near Rowe's desk.

Strong fingers brushed hair back from her face. "Go back to sleep," a deep voice urged her. "Go lay down in the bed this time, though."

She squinted against the sunlight pouring through a window high in the wall of the apartment that had been carved out of a corner of an abandoned airport hangar. "I can't sleep."

"You've been out for a couple of hours," he pointed out, his sexy mouth sliding into a crooked grin.

"I can't sleep now," she said with a shiver. "I have a really bad feeling."

Rowe came to her, lifting her from the chair only to settle back into it with her wrapped in his arms. "Sweetheart..."

Tears stung her eyes. "He's in too much danger— even more than he was in at Blackwoods. I'm afraid I'm never going to see my brother again."

Rowe said nothing, just tightened his strong arms around her and pressed a kiss to her forehead. She regretted now making him promise not to keep anything from her. She wished he could offer her some pretty lies that Jed was perfectly safe—that he would be fine and proven innocent soon.

She had spent the entire trial believing the fantasy that an innocent man wouldn't go to prison. Then she'd spent three years believing that his innocence would be revealed. She had wasted too much of her life believing that justice would win out. Now she knew better than anyone—but Jed—how unjust life could be.

But nothing would be more unjust than Jed dying a convicted killer. However, the sick feeling in her stomach worried her—that it was already too late for Jed to find the real killer. That eerie sense of foreboding that had jerked her awake had her convinced that the real killer had found Jed first.

FOR THREE YEARS, Jed had been locked into a six-by-six cage. He had been allowed out to eat in the cafeteria and to exercise in the prison yard. He hadn't been allowed to drive. But before his arrest, he'd been driving Humvees in Afghanistan.

The instincts that had aided him in avoiding ambushes and roadside bombs and had earned him that Purple Heart kicked in again. The minivan was no Humvee, but Jed—full of determination to protect his family as he had protected his men during their missions—steered it like it was one. He wrenched the wheel, driving into the skid across the slippery spring snow.

He avoided the deep ditches on the sides of the road, but metal crunched, bumpers connecting. The van slid again, still Jed held tight to the wheel and accelerated. This time the engine responded, kicking into a higher gear. But even with a working transmission, it couldn't outrun the more powerful car.

It drew alongside them, on the wrong side of the yellow line. Jed hoped like hell that someone came upon them from the other direction and sent that son of a bitch hurtling into the ditch.

Despite the fact that the sun had finally risen, it was too early for much traffic. Unfortunately, these were the only two vehicles on the road.

The black sedan was longer and heavier than the van, and its windows were tinted nearly as black as the rest of it. So, despite the morning sun that illuminated the inside of the van and Erica's beautiful face so pale with fear, Jed could not see inside the car.

He had no idea who was after them. The intruder from the apartment? An overly ambitious bounty hunter? Or the devil himself...

But then the passenger window of the car, which was on Jed's side, lowered. And he caught a glimpse of the driver.

His heart slammed into his ribs, and his hands shook so badly he nearly lost his grip on the steering wheel.

It couldn't be...

No, it's not possible.

He had gone too many days without sleep, so his mind was just playing tricks on him.

That had to be it...

But before Jed could determine whether or not he was hallucinating, the window rose back up.

And the car crashed into the side of the van, sending it spinning out of control...like Jed's imagination.

Chapter Ten

They weren't dead. Thanks to Jed. Erica didn't know how he had managed to keep the van from being totally submerged in the deep ditches on the side of the road. But he had avoided them as well as losing the car that had tried to run them off the road.

There had been no sight of the black vehicle behind them as they had traveled the rest of the way to Rowe Cusack's secret hideaway—an airplane hangar at an old private airstrip on the outskirts of Detroit.

At first she hadn't thought it was a meeting place. It seemed more like a means to escape to another country with no extradition. But no matter how much Jed trusted him, Rowe Cusack was still a lawman—who had vowed to uphold and not break the law. And there probably weren't many laws more severe to break than aiding a fugitive.

But she would learn the legalities for certain once she was caught. She had no illusions now that she wouldn't be. The prison van had been left in the alley behind her building, and Jed's fingerprints were all over her home.

And her body...

She tingled in remembrance of how they'd been touching each other before that news bulletin had interrupted them and they'd heard the sirens in the distance. They'd barely gotten out of Miller's Valley to avoid arrest. Heck, they'd barely gotten out of Miller's Valley alive, thanks to that black car.

She would love to go to that other country with no extradition. But no fueled plane awaited them as Jed pulled the van inside the nearly empty hangar. He stepped out of the van and came around, opening her door before sliding open the back door. A noise made him tense and turn toward the shadows inside the hangar.

Erica reached for their daughter, unbuckling her car seat to pull her into her arms. She clasped the child tight, willing to die to protect her.

"It's Rowe," Jed assured her.

A tall blond-haired man stepped out of the shadows where he must have been waiting to meet them, but he hadn't come alone. Instead of armed officers, only a dark-haired woman stood inside the hangar with the DEA agent.

The woman could have been an agent, too, but instead of drawing a weapon on Jed, she ran toward him with her arms outstretched. Jed met the woman, catching her up in his arms for a big hug.

Erica's chest felt tight, her heart compressed, as she watched their joyful reunion. This was the "she" that he'd promised would see him soon. The woman couldn't have met him while he was in prison, so she must have known him before and well enough to wait for him. And long enough that they would have already been involved before he'd slept with Erica the night their child had been conceived.

Erica clasped her arms more tightly around her daughter, who had somehow managed to fall asleep again after the excitement of their bumper car make-believe.

"Macy!" Jed exclaimed, his deep voice vibrating with joy and affection.

And Erica remembered him talking about this woman before, his voice vibrating then with love and pride. The tightness in her chest eased as she realized this was his sister.

Even though Erica had never met her, she should have recognized her. Not from the old picture Jed had shown her when they'd been going out before his deployment, or even from all the media coverage of her during the trial. Macy had given up her plans for medical school to aid her brother's appeal and release from prison. Erica should have recognized her because Isobel was a miniature replica of the young woman.

No wonder Jed had instinctively known, with nary a doubt nor demand for a DNA test, that Isobel was his daughter. It was very obvious that the little girl was this woman's niece.

Over her brother's massively broad shoulder, Macy caught sight of Erica and the unwieldy bundle in her arms. "Jed, who did you bring with you? Who is this?"

She pulled away from her brother and walked toward Erica. As her gaze focused on the sleeping child, her breath audibly caught.

"Is she my...?" Macy asked Erica, not her brother the question—more with her wide dark eyes than her words, which emotion had choked off.

Erica nodded, and the gesture must have shifted the little girl so that she awakened with a sleepy murmur of protest. "This is your niece, Isobel. Isobel, this pretty lady is your Aunt Macy."

"She is pretty," Isobel whispered in shy agreement.

"You're the pretty one," Macy said. "I am so happy to meet you." She held out her arms.

The little girl hesitated for just a moment before leaning toward her newly introduced aunt. Macy pulled her close, hugging her as tightly as she had her brother. Tears glistened in her eyes. "I was so worried I'd never see you again. But here you are and you're not alone…"

Jed approached, either to comfort his sister or explain. But the DEA agent intercepted him and led him off into another section of the hangar.

As if she had silently communicated with the blond man, Macy carried Isobel off toward an open door and stepped inside a room. Unwilling to be separated from her daughter again, Erica followed closely.

She gasped at the room in which they stood; it wasn't an office, as she would have expected. It was a studio apartment complete with kitchenette, skylights, queen-size bed and wall-unit furnace. "This is so nice."

"Not what you expected?" Macy asked.

"Nothing has been," Erica replied, "since Jed showed up at my door."

So many questions widened Macy's dark eyes, but she only remarked, "I can relate." She settled the little girl onto her hip as she reached into a cupboard and pulled down a box of crackers. "Are you hungry, sweetheart? What about you…?"

"Erica."

Macy's breath caught again. "Erica Towsley?"

"You know who I am?"

"I know Jed wanted Marcus to find you for the trial," she replied. "He never really told me why, though."

"He was with me the night of the murders," Erica admitted. "That was actually the night your niece was conceived."

Macy let out a whoop of excitement that had Isobel giggling. "That's it—the evidence we need to overturn his conviction."

Erica shook her head and, with regret, replied, "No. My memories of that night aren't very clear. They wouldn't hold up in court."

"But Isobel..."

"Is not proof that he never left—that he didn't do what he was convicted of."

Isobel hadn't asked about her daddy yet. Maybe she was too young and too sheltered in Miller's Valley to even realize that she didn't have one. But she actually did have one, and when she was old enough to ask about him—how ever would Erica explain why he hadn't been part of her life?

He couldn't go back to prison; he couldn't lose any more time with his daughter. The little girl deserved a father.

But, regrettably, Erica knew that life wasn't fair. And a child didn't always get what she deserved.

"He was framed," Macy maintained, as she resolutely had throughout his trial. "There has to be some way to prove that."

"Find out who framed him," Rowe said as he stepped inside the room with Jed.

Erica suspected Jed already knew. He had evaded that car that had been so determined to run them off the road. He had driven with the skill and composure that had had him surviving Afghanistan and probably prison, too.

But for just one moment he had lost it—when the car window had lowered. His broad shoulders and body had blocked her view, so Erica hadn't caught a glimpse of the driver. But Jed had.

She hadn't been able to question him about it yet, not with Isobel in the van with them. But confident Macy would care for her newly discovered niece, Erica stormed over to Jed and pulled him out into the hangar with her.

"You already know," she accused him. "You saw who was driving that car and you recognized him!"

He shook his head in denial, but he didn't meet her gaze.

She grasped his arm, and his muscles bunched beneath her fingers. She couldn't shake the truth out of him; he was too big. She could only demand he tell her. "Who was it? That monster tried to kill my daughter. I have a right to know who he is!"

Jed's dark eyes filled with torment and regret. "Erica…"

"Mommy?" The little girl must have wriggled free of her aunt, who stood in the doorway behind her, as Isobel ran to them. She squeezed between her father and mother and clung to Erica's legs. "I'm scared…"

Regret had nausea rising in Erica's throat as she realized that her daughter must have overheard her outburst. "You're safe, honey."

Jed's big hand cupped the back of their daughter's head. "You're safe, sweetheart," he assured the child. "I will protect you."

Because he knew what the threat was. Because he knew who it was…

JED HOPED HE HADN'T just made a promise he wouldn't be able to keep. He had seen the skepticism on Erica's lovely face. She didn't believe him. She didn't trust him. He didn't blame her. He stared after her as she carried their daughter back inside the studio apartment with his sister.

Rowe stayed behind, standing at Jed's side. Probably ready to slap the cuffs on him.

If he tried...

Well, Jed already knew he could take the Drug Enforcement Administration agent. Even though he didn't want to fight a man he now considered a friend, he would in order to keep his promise to Isobel. To protect her...and her mother.

"She seems to know you well," Rowe remarked, almost idly.

"If she knew me well, she wouldn't have spent the past three years thinking I'm a killer," Jed said, wondering if he would ever get over his bitterness and mistrust.

"But she was right that you did recognize the driver."

Jed shook his head, unable to believe what he'd seen hadn't been just his exhausted mind playing tricks on him. If he shared his suspicion with anyone, they'd lock him up for certain—in a sanatorium, though, instead of a prison. "No, she's wrong. I haven't slept in days. I could barely see the road, let alone his face."

Rowe uttered a heavy sigh of frustration and weariness. Dark circles rimmed the DEA agent's eyes. He had already tried talking to Jed once.

But he'd evaded Rowe's questions and insisted on checking on Erica and Isobel instead. After the harrowing trip away from Miller's Valley, he had wanted to make certain they were really all right.

He hadn't been convinced that Erica had allayed their daughter's fears despite her valiant attempts. She was an amazing mother. But Isobel was an intuitive child and had figured out that more was going on than a pretend game of bumper cars.

"Jedidiah," Rowe said, commanding his attention again, "I can't help you unless you tell me everything that you know."

"There's nothing to tell." Yet. "What about you? You got anything to tell me?"

"About the money?" Rowe asked. "I checked all her financial records. Erica Towsley doesn't have it."

Jed released a breath of relief. For three years he had believed she had betrayed him, and he'd hated her for it. And he'd hated himself for being a fool for her. It was good to know that he had been wrong about that. About her...

"A couple of years ago she inherited some money," Rowe continued, "a building and a bookkeeping business in a trust from an aunt, but there's no other money. She barely has enough to cover her expenses."

He had seen the building and the bookkeeping business on the main floor of it. It was nothing like the building Marcus Leighton had owned. As dilapidated as it was, she hadn't inherited much—more a money pit than a source of income.

"What about Leighton? Did you check his financials, too?"

"He got a chunk of change before your trial began and some mysterious deposits over the past three years," Rowe said, confirming his suspicions, "but not the amount that was embezzled from your clients and your firm before the murders."

"That money had to go somewhere..."

"I can't find it," Rowe said, frustration making his voice even raspier. "I've brought the records along with me, so you can go over them. That's your area of expertise, not mine."

"You track down drug money all the time, following it up the ladder to whoever's in charge." That was partially how the man had busted the warden of Blackwoods Penitentiary. The other part involved the hit the warden had put out on the DEA agent, ordering Jed to carry out that murder.

Rowe nodded in acceptance, not arrogance. "But this person's skills exceed mine. By far. Whoever hid those embezzled funds knows how to hide money where it won't ever be found."

Oh, God, it had to be…even though it made no sense, even though it wasn't possible…

"She's right and you're a damn liar," Rowe accused him, his eyes narrowed as he studied Jed's face. "You definitely know who the hell set you—"

Sirens saved Jed from uttering another lie. They echoed inside the hangar, bouncing off the tin walls and ceiling. Then the thump, thump, thump of helicopter blades drowned out the sirens.

Had Jed been a fool to trust this lawman? Had he been set up? And now, even before a voice announced it, he was surrounded with no means of escape.

JED PROBABLY THOUGHT he'd lost him. He ignored the quick sting to his pride. It didn't matter what Jed believed. It didn't even matter if he believed what he'd seen…

Nobody else would believe him if he shared his suspicions. It sounded crazy and would make Jed sound crazy. And the escaped convict would have no way of proving his suspicions.

He would make certain of that. He twisted a silencer

onto the end of his gun. All he had to do was wait for the perfect moment.

It would all be over soon.

No one else would know who was really responsible for Jedidiah Kleyn's tragic fall from hero to desperate convict but *him*.

And Jed...

Chapter Eleven

Was this how prison had felt for Jed?

Enclosed?

Tight?

Airless?

Erica had never realized she had issues with claustrophobia...until now. Thank God Isobel was safe with her aunt, and even though Erica had just met Macy, she knew the woman would protect her niece. While Erica worried about her child, she wouldn't have wanted her with her mother.

Erica was trapped beneath a grate in the cement floor, in a shallow drainage tunnel through which oil, gas and water ran from overhauled planes into holding tanks under the hangar.

But was it the small space in which she was confined or was it the man with whom she was confined that had her feeling panicked and overwhelmed?

Jed lay half-sprawled across her, as if shielding her with his body in case someone opened fire on them. But no one knew they were here...

"I know he's here," a deep male voice declared with absolute certainty.

"Sheriff York, you wasted your time coming all the way here from Blackwoods County," Rowe Cusack told the man. "And you wasted the time of all of these local officers you brought in as backup."

Fortunately the sheriff had already dismissed those officers after they had thoroughly searched the hangar. Or maybe not so thoroughly...

York pitched his voice lower when he replied, "I'm out of my jurisdiction, so I had to notify the local authorities that they potentially had one of the escaped convicts in their area."

"You should have let me handle this," a woman remarked with little respect for the sheriff's efforts. "Since I wouldn't have had to notify anyone. They overreacted and scared off the escapee before I had a chance to apprehend him."

"Ms. Franklin is a bounty hunter," Sheriff York explained to Rowe, his voice gruff with disdain. "She is the one that used some questionable measures to determine that you're helping Kleyn."

Rowe snorted loudly. "And you believed *a bounty hunter?*"

"On national television and to me personally, you admitted yourself that you think he's innocent," York said.

Erica had seen the DEA agent's interview replayed that morning when Jed had been in her room, watching their daughter sleep. Until then she hadn't seen the whole interview, just a few terse responses from the DEA agent to the reporters' incessant questions. He had been much more loquacious during his interview and had shared his opinion of Jed with the reporters.

"I do believe he's innocent," Rowe told the sheriff and the bounty hunter. "And I intend to prove his innocence so that his conviction gets overturned and he's released from prison."

"But first he has to go back to prison in order to be released," the sheriff pointed out, "so tell us where he is."

"Why do you think that Jedidiah Kleyn would come to me?" Rowe asked.

"Because you're dating his sister," the bounty hunter answered. Apparently it was no lie that she had some sources.

"I'm engaged to his sister," Rowe corrected her with obvious pride in his fiancée. "But I'm still a lawman. If Jed comes to me, I will bring him in to authorities myself."

Ms. Franklin snorted now as loudly—and unlady-like—as Rowe had. "Like your *fiancée* is going to allow that."

"My fiancée respects the law," Rowe replied, his voice deepening with the implication that the bounty hunter did not.

"Who's the kid she's hanging on to?" Ms. Franklin asked, prying for even more information. "I pulled up some information on Kleyn's sister and nothing ever mentioned her having a baby."

Over Jed's shoulder and through the thin slats of the grate, Erica discerned the shadow of the woman's arm pointing toward the room where Macy had stayed with Isobel while Mommy and her friend Jed "played hide-and-seek" with the police officers.

"But she looks just like your fiancée," the woman continued, "so she must be a relative."

Erica opened her lips, but before so much as even a gasp of fear could slip out, a big hand closed over her mouth. And Jed's face blocked her view of the grate, his eyes staring down into hers. With no words, he was asking her to trust him—that somehow, he would protect their daughter.

"She's proof that Jed's not here," Rowe said. "No one would want a child anywhere near a wanted man with a shoot-on-sight order out on him."

"That's not true," the sheriff said, quick to deny the claim.

"It may not be official, but it's true," Rowe insisted. "The governor put out the bounty on his head and someone else put out the shoot-on-sight order with a substantial reward offered for his death."

The sheriff sucked in a breath as if in acknowledgment of what the DEA agent claimed.

"He's right," the bounty hunter agreed. "There actually is a shoot-on-sight order out on this escaped convict. He killed a cop, man—"

"He didn't kill anyone." Rowe defended him, his voice rising in anger.

"He was convicted," Ms. Franklin stubbornly maintained, "so in everyone else's mind, that makes him guilty."

Jed's stare intensified, as if he was looking in Erica's eyes to see if she also found him guilty. While she had completely accepted his innocence of the crimes for which he'd been convicted, she couldn't trust that he hadn't changed in prison. That being sent there despite his innocence hadn't so embittered him that he wasn't an entirely different man from the one she'd fallen in love with so long ago.

"And a lot of people don't think that two lifetimes was a sufficient sentence for what he'd done," the bounty hunter said. "They think he deserved death."

"Michigan doesn't have the death penalty," Rowe reminded her.

She snorted again—even louder than before. "That's too bad."

Erica shivered at the woman's coldness. No doubt she would comply with the shoot-on-sight order if she actually caught sight of Jed. If Erica were stronger, she would have shifted them around, so that she was on top. But she wasn't big enough to hide Jed. She could only hope that the bounty hunter didn't look into the grate and discover them.

"Cusack's also right about not wanting the kid around," Ms. Franklin continued. "Kleyn might be monster enough to use a child as a shield..."

Jed's body had already been tense as he lay atop Erica, but now his muscles tightened more, as if he were struggling for control.

Was that why he had insisted that she and Isobel come along with him? Not to protect them but to protect himself?

To use his daughter as a shield...

A muscle twitched along his jaw, as if his control was slipping. Or as if he had read her reaction and knew that her doubts were back.

She had been a fool to trust him, though. A fool to come along with him. While it might not have been a good idea for her to wait for the police to show up at her apartment, especially given the way they had stormed the hangar, she could have taken Isobel someplace else. She had enough money in her account to hole up in hotels for a few nights.

The woman continued, "But I doubt Cusack here would do the same. Until this mess at Blackwoods, his record was exemplary."

"Still is," Rowe said. "Sheriff, you wasted your time and the officers' time in coming here."

"I don't think so," the sheriff replied. "I think you know a lot more than you're willing to admit."

"Yes," the bounty hunter agreed. "But he's not going to tell us anything."

"No." Rowe confirmed her accusation. "I'm not…"

"If you're aiding and abetting him, you're going to lose your job," the sheriff threatened, "and your freedom. Again."

According to what he had shared on the news broadcast, the DEA agent had been undercover at Blackwoods Penitentiary when his cover had been blown and someone had nearly killed him. So he knew what it was like to be locked up like Jed had been locked up the past three years.

"Don't worry about me," Rowe said. "Worry about catching all those escaped convicts. Kleyn isn't the only one, you know."

Several prisoners had broken out of Blackwoods Penitentiary during the riot—not just Jed, but Jed was the one everyone had focused on apprehending.

Or killing.

MACY COULDN'T STOP STARING at her brother's child— her niece. The little girl was so adorable. And smart. She'd said nothing when the officers had stormed the hangar. But her little chubby fingers had tightly gripped Macy's hand—as they did now while they waited to see if Mommy and her friend were discovered in their hiding place.

Her friend?

She didn't know Jed was her father. But then how would Erica Towsley have explained to the child why she couldn't see her daddy—because he was in prison for two murders.

Macy wanted Erica to explain some things to her, though, like why she hadn't come forward at Jed's trial. And why she had never let Jed know that he was a father. He couldn't have known before he'd broken out of prison, or he would have asked Macy to check on the little girl and her mother and make sure they were doing okay.

They weren't doing okay now. Just by being with Jed, they were in danger. Those local officers had all had their guns drawn until Sheriff York had ordered them holstered. If he hadn't been present, she was certain shots might have been fired.

And if Jed was discovered hiding in that grate, she suspected that shots might still be fired.

Macy lifted the child in her arms and turned away from the window that looked onto the rest of the hangar. She couldn't protect her brother now—not if the sheriff and the bounty hunter found him.

But she would protect his daughter. She didn't want the little girl to witness the executions of her parents…

EVEN AFTER THE HANGAR DOOR slid closed again, Jed held his breath. Rowe might not have really convinced the sheriff and the bounty hunter to leave. They might have only pretended to accept his claims and could be waiting for Jed to step out of his hiding place.

If he had been alone, waiting them out would have been no problem. He'd waited three years for the opportunity to prove his innocence. And those three years had been spent in a hole far worse than this hiding place.

The reason it was so hard to wait was Erica. She lay under him, her body soft and warm beneath his. Her face was so close to his that all he had to do was turn his head slightly to skim his lips across hers. But he wanted more than her kiss.

More even than her body.

He wanted her trust, too. And those damn doubts were back in her eyes, as clear as the sky-blue color that had haunted him the past three years. Everything about Erica Towsley had haunted him the past three years. Maybe she had been duped into doubting him once. But if she had really cared about him, she would not have been so easily fooled…

"I think they're gone," she whispered, her warm breath feathering across his cheek. And then she squirmed, her hips arching against his.

He swallowed a groan, as his body reacted—hardening and demanding release. Desire hammered at him, pulsing in his veins and tightening all his muscles. They had nearly made love earlier, at her apartment, until the breaking-news bulletin had returned them to their senses. Now the sound of shoes scraping across the cement floor above them drew Jed back to reality.

He couldn't make love to Erica here. He couldn't make *love* to Erica anywhere because he could never love a woman who did not believe in him. Having everyone but Macy turn on him and look at him with fear and disgust had destroyed something inside him— his self-respect and maybe his own ability to trust.

And to love.

As he had earlier, he covered her mouth with his hand—holding back any gasps or words she might have inadvertently uttered. Anyone could have stepped back inside the hangar.

Her breath warmed his palm and had a tingling sensation shooting up his arm—straight to his heart. The damn woman affected him as no other ever had. If only she could have loved him…

But she hadn't had enough faith in him to have had any real feelings for him.

"They're really gone," Rowe said. He knelt beside the drainage tunnel and pulled up the grate. "I waited and watched to make certain that they drove away."

"And knowing you, you probably threw out a few threats and a couple more lies," Jed said. He tried to get up, but he didn't want to put any more of his weight on Erica

Rowe reached down and offered him a hand up. As Jed grabbed it and hauled himself to his feet, Rowe said, "I wasn't lying to the sheriff."

He had to force it, but Jed grinned at the DEA agent's semantics. "You didn't tell him that I was here."

"That was an omission," Rowe clarified.

To pretty much everybody else and most especially Jed, a lie of omission was still a lie. Erica not coming forward to alibi him was a lie of omission he might never be able to forgive.

"I was telling the truth about bringing you in, though," Rowe warned him.

Jed nodded. "Of course you will—once I go through the financial records from my and Brandon's accounting firm, and I have the evidence I need to prove my innocence. Then you'll bring me in until my conviction can be overturned."

That didn't guarantee his immediate release, though. He would have to do jail time for breaking out of prison. But until he had found out about Isobel, he hadn't cared that he would have to go back…because he'd known it was for a crime he had actually committed. And then everyone would know the truth—that he wasn't a killer.

Jed turned back to Erica, reaching one hand down to help her from the tunnel. But the hole was shallow so she was already hauling herself up the cement side.

Cold metal encircled his wrist and then snapped tight around it. The sensation was horribly familiar.

Rowe dragged his other hand behind his back and manacled it, too. "No, Jed, I have to bring you in *now*. I have to arrest you for breaking out of prison. I have to bring you back."

"Back to Blackwoods?"

Back to Hell?

"There isn't much left of Blackwoods," Rowe reminded him. "It'll take them years to rebuild that prison. Your name will be clear for a long time before the construction is done on Blackwoods Penitentiary. You'll never have to go back there."

"I won't have the chance," Jed said. "Once you take me in, I'm a dead man. And I'm going to die a guilty man, convicted of crimes I never committed."

And worse than that, he finally had an idea who was really responsible for those crimes. But until he could prove it, nobody would believe him. However, he wouldn't be able to prove anything if he was behind bars or dead. "Don't do this, Rowe..."

"I have no choice," he replied, all DEA agent now instead of friend and future brother-in-law. "I'm putting you under arrest..."

"You're putting me six feet under..."

He was definitely a dead man.

Chapter Twelve

"He's arresting him," Erica whispered, as she stared through the window that looked onto the hangar. Her stomach clenching with dread and fear, she was as horrified now as she had been when Rowe Cusack had first slapped the cuffs on Jed.

But before he could drag him off, Macy had rushed out and joined them. Instead of staying there to support Jed, Erica had hurried toward her daughter. She hadn't wanted Isobel to see any more than she already had. So she'd caught the child up in her arms and carried her back inside the apartment.

"You played hide 'n' seek real good, Mommy," Isobel praised her. "Nobody found you."

Too bad Rowe had known where they were…

Not that she had wanted to stay inside that tunnel with Jed forever. The confinement had been overwhelming or maybe that had just been her feelings—her desire—for the man that had overwhelmed her. Being too close to Jed made her lose her objectivity and her common sense. Maybe it wouldn't be bad if Rowe took him back to jail as long as he could keep him safe.

But she doubted anyone could guarantee Jed's safety now. Too many people wanted him dead.

"Is it my turn to play hide 'n' seek now?" Isobel

asked. "I want Jed to be my partner." The little girl followed Erica's gaze out the window and wrinkled her nose in confusion. "Is he playing a game with that other man now?"

She wished it was just a game. Apparently so did Macy as she yelled at her fiancé. They were too far away for Erica to hear the words she shouted, but her argument must have been effective because he removed the handcuffs.

When Erica had been out there with them, she had heard his words and knew the DEA agent had spoken them with grim determination. He didn't like this part of his job, but he wasn't able to ignore his duty to uphold the law. Rowe Cusack was definitely going to bring Jed back to prison.

"I guess they are playing a game." One neither man really wanted to play, though.

The little girl yawned. "I'm kind of sleepy now. I can hide 'n' seek with Jed later."

The child hadn't really had much sleep—at least uninterrupted sleep—since Jed had shown up at their door.

Erica hugged her daughter, holding her close and rocking her back and forth in her arms. She was already comforting her because, if Jed went back to prison, the child wasn't going to be able to seek out her father for a while.

Maybe never.

"Damn him!" Macy said, as she stepped back inside and slammed the door shut. Horror and regret widened her eyes, and she lowered her voice. "I'm so sorry. I forgot all about…"

Her niece.

But then, she had just become aware of the child's existence. "It's okay," Erica assured her. "Isobel can sleep through anything."

"I've heard kids are resilient," Macy remarked with obvious envy. She crossed the room to the brass bed near the fireplace and dragged back the blankets. "You can lay her down here."

Erica followed Macy to the bed, but she hesitated before releasing her daughter. If the police had discovered Jed and her hiding beneath that grate, she could have lost her child forever.

Macy reached out and squeezed Erica's shoulder. "She's safe here. I would never let anything happen to her," she promised. "I would never let anyone take her or hurt her."

Had Jed told her about the man in her apartment? If Isobel hadn't awakened and gone with Mrs. Osborn to her place, that man might have taken Isobel.

"I'm her mother. I'm supposed to be the one to protect her," Erica said, feeling as though she'd failed miserably.

"She's a happy, healthy little girl, so you obviously have protected her all of her life," Macy said. "But I want to help you now."

"Why?" Erica asked, confused that a virtual stranger could be so generous. "You don't even know us."

Macy moved her hand from Erica's shoulder to Isobel's cheek. "She's my niece. My brother's daughter..." Her voice cracked as emotion overwhelmed her. "When I was growing up, Jed was always there for me—giving me the love and support our parents couldn't give me. I failed Jed when it mattered most. I wasn't able to save him from prison. Three years ago—" she glanced out the window and bit her lip "—or now."

"You got Rowe to take off the handcuffs," Erica

pointed out. And the DEA agent hadn't put them back on yet.

"I talked him out of arresting Jed in front of his daughter," Macy said.

When Erica finally settled Isobel onto the bed, Macy's breath caught as if she feared that her fiancé had been waiting for just that moment before he hauled her brother off to prison again.

"Rowe can't take him in," Erica said. All those claims the bounty hunter had made rushed back to her, bringing fear and panic. "He'll die in custody."

Because every law-enforcement officer wanted him dead out of vengeance over the death of the young cop. Apparently officers never forgot a fallen comrade.

Macy shook her head, unwilling or unable to consider how much danger her brother was in. "Jed survived three years in the most dangerous prison in Michigan."

"And maybe that's how he survived," Erica pointed out. "Maybe his label of cop killer actually protected him inside the corrupt jail. But now…"

Macy's breath shuddered out in a shaky sigh. "Now he'll be sent somewhere else until we can find the real killer and clear his name."

"Jed knows who the killer is." Even though he wouldn't admit it. And why wouldn't he admit it? Was he actually protecting the real guilty person? Or was he protecting everyone else he cared about? Everyone else but himself…

"Damn it, Rowe, you can't bring me in now." Not when he was so close to proving his innocence. All he had to do was prove his sanity—to himself—first.

Rowe glanced toward the window leading to that

little apartment inside the hangar. "I know it has to be damn hard, just finding out you have a kid and having to leave her again. But, Jed, I can't have you out here— at the mercy of every bounty hunter and cop with a grudge."

"I'll be even more at their mercy when I'm locked up," Jed argued. "You were in there—you know what it's like."

"That was Blackwoods and Blackwoods is gone. And Warden James will probably be locked up for the rest of his life."

Jed snorted in derision.

"The D.A. made sure his bail was denied," Rowe said, "he's not getting out."

"Not now but anything could happen at his trial." No one knew that better than him. He had been so convinced that he wouldn't be convicted of crimes he hadn't committed. He'd been so naïve. "Plenty of guilty people have gotten off." Especially if Jed wasn't alive to testify against him.

Rowe shook his head, unwilling to believe it. "Not James. He's guilty as hell."

"And I was innocent. You can't trust that the justice system is going to work." There were times a man needed to take justice into his own hands. And if Jed was right about who had set him up, he would mete out his own justice to the bastard who had stolen three years of his life.

Rowe must have misunderstood what justice system Jed was talking about because he asked, "You really think you'll be in danger in jail?"

"You were the first one who warned me about the shoot-on-sight order out on me," Jed reminded him. "And now the governor put a big bounty on my head.

Do you really think I will ever make it out to see my daughter again?"

"Jed..." Rowe narrowed his eyes with suspicion, as if he thought Jed was deliberately playing on his emotions.

Maybe he was. "I can't go back inside until I find the evidence that'll clear me."

"I'll find it," Rowe assured him.

"*You* don't know where to look." He wasn't sure that he did, either.

How did one go about tracking down a ghost?

"So Erica's right." Rowe cursed him. "You did recognize the person who tried to force you off the road on your way here."

He shrugged. "It's probably the same person who broke into her apartment. If Isobel hadn't been across the hall at the neighbor's who was watching her, she might not be here with us."

"You don't have to be out of prison to be able to protect her," Rowe said. "I will protect her for you. I'll make sure no one threatens or hurts that little girl."

Some of the weight on his shoulders eased. "I'm counting on that."

"You have my promise."

Jed nodded in acceptance. He knew the DEA agent didn't give his promise lightly and that once he did, he kept it. Or Macy wouldn't be here yet. Rowe had promised to protect Jed's little sister, and that was a vow he had nearly died to keep. "Thank you."

Rowe drew in an audibly ragged breath. "So I'll take you in now. And I'll make sure that nothing happens to you in custody."

"I'm not going in," Jed argued, desperation clawing

at him. "I have to dig up more information to prove my innocence."

"Tell me, and I'll get it for you," Rowe offered.

"Did you find the witnesses from my trial? Brandon's girlfriend?" She was the key.

"The last person you believe really saw your business partner alive," Rowe replied, almost as if stalling for time before divulging, "She's dead."

Damn it all...

"She was murdered." Like Marcus Leighton, she'd been a loose end that needed tying up.

"Her death was ruled a suicide," Rowe said. "She hung herself shortly after the trial. Maybe the guilt over lying on the stand..."

Jed shook his head. That woman had felt no guilt; in fact she'd almost been gleeful when she'd testified, as if she'd been privy to a big joke that no one else had known. "I'd like you to look into it more. I think she was murdered, like my lawyer."

Rowe studied him for a moment before nodding in agreement. "Okay. I'll have the investigation reopened. I'll take a look at the autopsy report myself. If she was murdered, we'll find out."

"What about the other witness—the man who testified to my killing the cop?" Jed asked. "Is he dead, too?"

Rowe shook his head. "No."

Not yet. But Jed had a bad feeling that if they didn't get to him soon—it would be too late. "Do you know where he is?"

Rowe nodded. "I intend to go see him as soon as I guarantee that you'll be safe in jail."

Jed shook his head. "That's a guarantee you'll never

get until I'm proved innocent. Let me prove my innocence, Rowe."

"How?" the lawman asked. "By threatening the witness? That'll just get you in more trouble."

"I can't get in more trouble than I already am," Jed pointed out.

"You can get dead just like Marcus Leighton and that female witness," Rowe warned him. "The real killer is out there and determined to cover his tracks, Jed. You're in danger from him, too."

"If this guy wanted me dead, he wouldn't have gone to the trouble of framing me for crimes I didn't commit," Jed reasoned. "He would have just killed *me*." That would have been far more merciful than ruining his reputation and then his life.

"*Whoever* this guy is—" Rowe rolled his eyes "—and I'm with Erica that you know his identity or at least strongly suspect, he really hates you or he wouldn't have wanted you sent away to prison for life."

"Two lifetimes," Jed reminded him of his sentence. That sick psycho had given him two lives; now maybe he would try to take two lives. He glanced toward the hangar apartment but could only see Macy inside. Maybe Erica had been so exhausted from her sleepless night that she'd lain down with their daughter. "You have to protect Erica and Isobel."

"They are in danger," Rowe agreed. "We all are for helping you. If anyone can prove that we have…"

He swallowed hard. Mrs. Osborn might testify against Erica, saying that she had claimed him as an old friend. No matter if he proved his innocence of the original charges, he had still broken out of jail and she had still helped him. He would do what he could to protect them. He would claim that he'd forced her to help him, but nobody had believed him when he'd professed his own innocence. Why would they believe him when he professed hers?

"Let me get the hell out of here. Then you can get Isobel and Erica away, too," he suggested. "You need to take them someplace where no one can find them."

As his trial had proven, anyone could get bought off. Lawyers, witnesses...probably police officers could, too. He had learned to trust no one but Macy. And because of Jed's love and devotion to her, the DEA agent was an extension of his sister.

Rowe shook his head as if denying his request. But then he groaned and said, "I'm a damn fool for going along with this."

"Not arresting me will make Macy happy," Jed reminded him.

"Your getting killed will make her hate me." Rowe's throat rippled as he swallowed hard. "Forever."

"That's a good reason for my not going to jail until I can prove I was framed."

"I'm not as worried about that shoot-on-sight order as I am about you confronting a killer all by yourself, Jed. I'll go with you."

"No." He rejected the DEA agent's suggestion. "I need you to take care of them."

Rowe shook his head. "You don't need me to do that. Your sister is pretty formidable."

"I wouldn't put my sister in that kind of danger. She's not formidable enough to handle this guy without getting hurt or killed," Jed warned him. "This man is more devious and more powerful than even Warden James. He has to be stopped."

The thought of his fiancée in danger had Rowe reaching for the tense muscles in the nape of his neck, just below his blond hair. "And you think you're the only one who can stop this monster?"

"I know I am," Jed confirmed.

Rowe shook his head in disbelief—not in what Jed had claimed but apparently over what he had decided. "There's a car in the back of the hangar under a bunch of tarps. The plate and the vehicle identification numbers are untraceable. Use it and get the hell out of here before I change my mind."

Jed didn't say goodbye to anyone but Rowe. He didn't step back inside that apartment to kiss his sister goodbye or take one last look at his daughter. And Erica.

If he had, he might not have left.

And he had to leave to keep them safe.

WARDEN JAMES KEPT HIS EYES closed but his ears opened. He wasn't the only one disgusted with the new sheriff. The jail guards weren't happy with him, either—especially as he kept running off to chase down escaped convicts and came back with precious few.

He wouldn't have to worry about York much longer. The mayor would probably call a special meeting with the town council and have him recalled. And thankfully, he probably wouldn't have to worry about Jedidiah Kleyn much longer, either.

Sure, the sheriff wasn't wrong about Kleyn being hard to kill. But then, probably not even in Afghanistan had the man ever had as many people gunning for him then as he had now.

It was just a matter of time before he turned up. Dead.

And then the case against Jefferson would die, too, when the only witness against him, who hadn't benefited from his crimes, was gone.

Jefferson hoped that eventually it was discovered who really committed the murders for which Kleyn had been convicted. Because he wanted to shake that guy's hand...

THE MORE DISTANCE JED PUT between himself and his family the easier he breathed. The pressure, over his mere presence putting them in danger, eased off his chest.

Just over a week ago, Rowe had promised to protect Macy from the fallout of helping the DEA agent escape from Blackwoods and the hit the warden had put on him. Rowe had kept that promise, but as he'd said, Macy was formidable. She could defend herself.

Could Erica defend herself, if she had to? She had been stubborn with him when she'd insisted on going along to see Leighton. But was she strong enough to fight for her life and their daughter's life if she had to?

He didn't have to worry about her, though. She and Isobel were safe with Rowe and Macy. He expelled a ragged breath of relief and heard an echoing gasp from the backseat.

His muscles tightened in reaction. He wasn't alone. For three years, in the most dangerous prison in Michigan, he hadn't let anyone get a jump on him.

Ever.

Just a few days out of prison and already his reflexes had dimmed. But the car had been covered with all those tarps, so he hadn't thought to check to see if anyone had crawled inside. The windows were all tinted, so he hadn't even been able to see into the backseat. And peering into the rearview mirror revealed nothing.

Had he imagined the sound? His gut told him no. Every nerve taut with awareness, he knew he wasn't alone.

He doubted it was the sheriff. The man would have shown himself before now, before Jed had gotten so many miles away from the hangar.

Unless that was what he'd been waiting for—distance and seclusion so that no one would witness him gun down the escaped convict—the cop killer—in cold blood.

If distance and seclusion was what the *law*man wanted, Jed would make sure he got it. He pulled off the two-lane highway onto what looked like a two-track that probably led to someone's seldom-used cottage or maybe to an abandoned oil well.

At least he hoped the road was seldom used because he didn't want his stowaway calling in reinforcements. Jed wasn't about to go out without a fight...

Chapter Thirteen

It wasn't Jed that had made Erica feel panicky earlier in the confined space. And even though she was wedged in tight behind some seats and covered with a dusky, mildew-smelling tarp, it wasn't the confined space either that had her so scared. It was the fear of being caught.

If only the tarp wasn't so thick, it would have been easier for her breathe. But it was also so foul-smelling that she'd been compelled to hold her breath until she'd had to gasp for more.

Had he heard her?

Was that why he had pulled onto some bumpy road? Or was he just following the directions Rowe had given him to the witness's house? If so, that man hadn't received the payout that Marcus Leighton had. Or maybe he had already drunk or drugged his way through whatever money he had received to perjure himself on the stand.

She bounced against the floorboards as the car hit every rut. Her elbow knocked against the metal bracket that fastened the driver's seat to the floor, and her fingers tingled and went numb. She swallowed a curse at the pain. She had to stay as quiet as possible.

The car stopped, sparing her any more abuse from the bumps. The driver's door opened and slammed closed. Maybe this wasn't the witness's house. Maybe this was actually where the man Jed had recognized driving the car lived.

Anxious to see, she closed her fingers over the edge of the tarp. But before she could pull it away from her face, the back door opened. Through the heavy canvas, big hands grasped her legs and dragged her from the floor. Her head struck the metal opening of the door, then gravel bit into her back as she dropped to the ground.

"It's me," she said, but the heavy canvas muffled her voice.

And what if it wasn't Jed?

What if they hadn't really lost that man in the black sedan and he had returned and run Jed off onto the bumpy road? She reached in her pocket for the weapon Macy had pressed into her hand earlier. She hadn't wanted it; she had been more concerned about hurting herself with it. But now she unsheathed the blade and hacked at the heavy canvas, trying to cut through the tarp to defend herself.

A man cursed, but his voice was muffled, just as hers undoubtedly was to him. She couldn't yell out his name, though, because what if it was the police or maybe that husky-voiced female bounty hunter who had pulled him over? Then they would know she was willingly with him.

She would not willingly go with them. She pushed the scalpel through the canvas again and elicited another curse from the man. It was definitely a man—not the female bounty hunter.

Then the tarp lifted, as he pulled it off her face and body. She rolled with it, coming up on her side with the hand holding the scalpel trapped beneath her body.

The blade nipped through her heavy jeans and nicked her hip.

She gasped at the little stab of pain and tried to roll off the weapon. But a foot was on her other shoulder, shoving her into the ground. She turned her head toward her attacker. And she gasped again. Fear had her heart racing as she stared up at the look of intense rage on his face.

She had thought she would only be in danger if it was someone other than Jed who had dragged her from her hiding place. Now she wasn't so sure. He looked as though he intended to kill her.

He cursed her but lifted his foot from her shoulder. "What the hell are you doing here?"

"What I should have done three years ago," she said. "Help you prove your innocence."

He reached a hand down toward her to bring her upright, and blood dripped from his fingers.

"Oh, my God, I hurt you."

He nodded in agreement, but she suspected he referred to more than the shallow wound on the back of his hand. The canvas must have taken the brunt of the blade. She'd hurt him more with her doubts than she ever could have with the scalpel.

"'Least I don't have to worry about you being able to defend yourself," he remarked as he smeared his blood off on his jeans.

Erica had been worried that she wouldn't be able to use the weapon even if she needed it. So pride overtook the twinge of guilt she felt for hurting him. "Your sister gave it to me."

He nodded. "I figured that out. What I can't figure out is why you're here. Why aren't you with our daughter and Macy and Rowe?"

"She's safe with them." She truly believed that Macy and Rowe would protect her little girl as if Isobel were their own. Or she never would have left her precious baby with them.

"I know that," he agreed. "That's why I asked Rowe to protect her." He stepped closer and pushed her tangled hair back from her face. "I also asked him to protect you. By letting you get into this car, he broke his promise to me."

She shook her head. "Rowe doesn't know I climbed into the back."

"It was my sister's idea?"

"It was mine," she corrected him. "Macy only mentioned the car when it looked as though Rowe wasn't going to arrest you. She'd hoped that he'd brought the car there for you to use as an escape vehicle."

"Yeah, some escape," he said, his voice gruff with irony.

"You wanted to escape from me, too?" she asked. "You tracked *me* down." Something she hadn't thought he would be able to do, or she would have hidden from him the moment she'd learned of the prison break. But then she might have never learned the truth. And she needed that knowledge—for Isobel. So the little girl learned the truth about her father instead of the lies everyone else—including Erica—had believed.

"That was because I thought you could help me," he reminded her.

She flinched that all he had wanted from her was an alibi. But then, what could she expect from him after he had spent the past three years believing she'd betrayed him?

"I can help you." She could stop him from doing something he would live to regret. As she'd snuck out to the car, she had overheard his conversation with Rowe and knew that Jed was on his way to talk to the remaining witness. Or threaten that witness as he had probably intended to threaten Marcus Leighton.

Or was that just what he had told Rowe so that the DEA agent wouldn't suspect that he was on his way to confront the real killer?

Rowe might have been willing to trust Jed to go off alone, but she couldn't. Her silence might have cost him three years of his life; she wasn't going to be silent again while he wound up serving more jail time.

"You can't help me," Jed insisted. "You're just going to get in my way."

As she suspected, he was going after the real killer—not the witness. "Jed, you can't do this alone."

He shook his head. "I can't do this with you."

"I can take care of myself," she reminded him.

"A scalpel isn't going to save you from a bullet," he pointed out. "And no one's going to save you from me."

Erica gasped at his ominous tone. She lifted her gaze to his face. He had that intense look again—the one that had her fearing for her safety. She'd hidden in the vehicle because she had been afraid for Jed. Now she was afraid of him...

Her eyes widened and all the color left her beautiful face; she was scared of him. He should have felt satisfaction since that was what he'd wanted. But regret clutched his heart.

He had so many regrets where Erica Towsley was concerned. And now he was about to have another. He reached for her, dragging her up against his body, which was hard with desire for her.

She was still hanging on to the scalpel; she could

have used it on him. He wouldn't have blamed her since he'd intended to deliberately frighten her.

And maybe he had intended this kiss to scare her, too, because he started out rough. He pressed his mouth tightly against hers, forcing her lips apart for the bold invasion of his tongue.

She gasped for breath and lifted her hands to his shoulders. Instead of pushing him away, she clutched him closely and moaned. Her reaction snapped his control. He didn't care that she was scared of him and that she didn't trust him; all he cared was that she wanted him, too.

He pulled her down to the ground with him, releasing her only long enough to spread the heavy tarp across the dirt path next to the car. Despite the trees that densely lined both sides of the two-track lane, the sun had melted whatever snow had fallen here. That bright sun had also warmed the day so that it felt like spring again—fresh and full of promise.

They had once had that promise before he'd gotten the orders calling him back to active duty and deploying him overseas. Their instant attraction and emotional connection had been so strong.

Maybe it was because he'd been locked up for three years, but that attraction felt even stronger now. He couldn't fight it. And she wasn't fighting him.

Instead she was lying down beside him on the tarp. Her hands ran up his chest, her palm settling against his pounding heart. Maybe she'd wondered if he still had one.

He was actually kind of surprised that he had; he'd thought he had lost it three years ago. He'd thought she'd stolen it and stomped all over it. He wanted her. But he wouldn't give her his heart again. He didn't trust her any more than she trusted him.

"Why?" he asked her.

"Why what?"

"Why aren't you fighting me?" he wondered aloud. "Why aren't you jabbing that scalpel into my chest?"

She shivered. "Should I be fighting you? Are you going to hurt me?"

He had to answer her honestly. "Probably."

IF HE HAD LIED TO HER—if he'd made her promises that they both knew he might not be able to keep—she would have pulled away from him. But his honesty increased her desire for him. And she'd already never wanted anyone—even him—more.

He still scared her, but what she felt for him frightened her more. She couldn't fall for a man she didn't even know anymore...if she'd ever really known him at all. Before she'd gotten the chance to really know him, he had pushed her away and left her for war. Then he'd only been back a short while before he'd left her for prison.

She knew she would never be able to keep him, but she wanted these stolen moments off the beaten track. So she clenched her hands in his shirt and dragged it over his head.

Sunlight shone through the trees and shimmered off his massively muscled chest. Her breath caught in appreciation and desire. But she had barely a moment to enjoy the sight of him before he pushed off her coat and pulled her shirt over her head.

"Are you cold?" he asked, dragging her tight against his naked chest.

Heat flushed her skin, which tingled everywhere she touched him. "No…"

Then he was kissing her again—deeply, his tongue sliding through her lips and over her tongue. She could taste him and feel him. And she wanted him too much to feel anything but desire. She certainly didn't notice the cold.

Her fingers trembled as she reached for the snap of his jeans, pulling it loose. Then his hands replaced hers, and he shucked off his jeans. She fumbled with her own snap, but his hands were there, too, pulling off the rest of her clothes.

Cool air rushed over her, raising goose bumps on her skin. He cursed and rubbed his palms over her arms and then her breasts. "You are cold."

Her nipples peaked, and tension wound tight inside her. She moaned, and he replaced his hands with his lips, tugging at one of her nipples until she whimpered with desire.

Her hands were busy, too, sliding over all his smooth skin. Muscles rippled beneath her touch. She ran her fingertips down his back to his butt.

He groaned against her breast. "Erica…"

"I want you…" She shouldn't. She had so many reasons not to trust him. Not to want him. But she wanted him.

Her admission snapped his control because he pushed her back onto the tarp. And his mouth went crazy, covering every inch of her with kisses that heated her skin. When his mouth slid lower, between her legs, she arched off the tarp. She shuddered with ecstasy and screamed his name.

And then he was there, filling her. She had forgotten how big he was. She stretched and arched, trying to take him deep inside her.

He held most of his weight onto his arms, the muscles flexing and bulging. She slid her hands over them and then over her shoulders to his back. She wrapped her arms and legs around him, holding on to him as tightly as she could for as long as she could.

She had no illusions that it would be long. But she would enjoy it while she could. She kept arching into him, meeting his thrusts.

He sank deeper and deeper into her. And that pressure that had wound so tight inside her finally broke free. She screamed his name as pleasure overwhelmed her.

Then, with a deep guttural groan, he joined her in ecstasy. His big body shuddered, but instead of dropping on top of her, he rolled to his side. Then he pulled her tight against him.

His hand ran up and down her back. "You're cold..."

Sweat beaded on her lip, but the wind was chilling her skin.

He grabbed up their clothes and arranged them over her. Something scratched her hip and she flinched, fearing the scalpel had found her again. But when she tentatively reached out, she realized it was car keys that had fallen out of his pocket.

"Sleep," he urged her. "You were up all night."

"So were you," she said. And she suspected that hadn't been the only night's sleep he'd missed. "Are you going to sleep, too?"

"I haven't really slept since before the riot," he admitted. But from the tension in his big body, she doubted that he would be able to sleep even now.

She was pretty certain that he had a plan. And he

wouldn't sleep until he saw the plan through. She wondered now how much that plan was about clearing his name and how much about vengeance.

She had to stop him from doing something that would put him back in prison for good. But she couldn't stay awake; her eyelids had grown too heavy to keep open. She would close them for just a minute.

Just a minute...

But when she awoke what might have been only moments later, she was alone.

WHERE THE HELL WAS JED? Had prison slowed down the man? From the skirmish in Erica Towsley's apartment, he knew Jed hadn't physically slowed. But maybe prison had dulled his usually quick mind. He should have been here by now. For most of their lives, Jed had been ahead of him—in class, in accolades.

Except for the past three years.

Then Jed had fallen behind. He hadn't been smart enough or fast enough to figure out how he had been framed or who had done it to him.

Now that Jed had seen *him* behind the wheel of the car that had nearly driven his family off the road, Kleyn knew the truth.

But he would never be able to prove it. No one would. No, Jed would die before he would ever be able to prove his innocence.

He would die a guilty man—as soon as he stepped into the trap that had been set for him.

Chapter Fourteen

Leaving her alone had been so hard. But Jed had
wrapped her in her clothes and the tarp to keep her
warm. He had also left her the drop cell phone Rowe
had given him. He suspected the DEA agent had a GPS
on it, so he would find Erica.

Hopefully before it grew dark.

Could he leave her alone?

He had yet to start the car and drive off. He hadn't
even shut the driver's door because he hadn't wanted to
awaken her. The engine would when he started it, but
by then it would be too late for her to catch him.

He drew in a deep breath and reached for the keys.
But they didn't dangle from the ignition. He must have
taken them with him when he'd jumped out of the car.
So he searched his pockets. They were empty.

Where the hell were the keys?

Metal creaked as she pulled open the passenger door
and settled onto the seat. She held the keys out between
them. "Looking for these?"

Back when they had first met, he had admired her
quick brain. She had been applying for a job with his
firm, and he'd wanted to hire her. But he had wanted
to date her even more. When he'd told her that, she had
willingly withdrawn her application. She'd already had a

job with her aunt's bookkeeping firm in Miller's Valley, but she had wanted to move to a bigger city. She had wanted more opportunities than Miller's Valley had offered.

She had found another job in Grand Rapids. And he had found her.

"Erica…"

"I can't believe you were going to leave me alone here in the middle of nowhere," she said, glaring at him—her blue eyes icy with fury and hurt.

"I left you Rowe's cell phone," he pointed out. It protruded from the front pocket of her jeans.

She nodded. "I don't have a clue where I am, though."

"He would have found you." He swallowed hard. "He *will* find you."

"You're going to throw me out of the car?"

"I can't bring you with me." He wasn't going to talk to just the witness. There was someone else he was determined to find—unless he was just chasing a ghost.

"Why not?" she asked, but she gave him no chance to answer. "It's not because you're going to talk to the witness. It's because you don't want any witnesses when you settle the score with whoever framed you."

"I don't want you getting hurt." So maybe he shouldn't have made love with her. But he suspected he would be the one who got hurt over that, over letting down his guard enough to get that close to a woman he would never be able to trust. Any more than she trusted him…

She shook her head, rejecting his claim. "You don't think I'll get hurt with you leaving me in the middle of nowhere?"

"Rowe will find you," he insisted, reaching for the keys.

She pulled them back, holding them near the passenger's door. "But will *he* find me first?"

Jed's arms were longer than hers, his grip stronger, so he easily reached across her and took the keys from her. But then he replayed her comment in his head. "What do you mean?"

"That man who broke into my apartment—the man you recognized but won't admit that you did—he could find me before Rowe gets here."

His breath stuck in his lungs for a moment, then escaped in a ragged sigh. "Damn it…"

She was right. If she hadn't stolen the keys from his pocket, he might have left her at the mercy of a maniac. Sure, he'd been watching his rearview mirror and hadn't noticed anyone following him. But then he hadn't noticed her in the backseat, either.

He could have a missed a tail. The sheriff or the bounty hunter or maybe the killer himself if he hadn't already bought off someone else to do his dirty work as he had last time. "I need to talk to the witness."

He needed to learn what the man had really seen that night so that Jed would know if he could trust that what he'd seen hadn't been just a figment of his overexhausted mind.

"You're going to have to take me with you," she stubbornly insisted as she buckled herself into the passenger seat.

She was right. He couldn't leave her here. But he worried that bringing her along might put her in more danger than leaving her behind.

NOT ONLY HAD SHE GRABBED his keys but she'd grabbed up the scalpel again, too. It was sheathed and inside her pocket. The slight weight of it against her hip comforted her. It was the only comfort she had as Jed remained silent and tense behind the steering wheel.

Not many more miles passed from the two-track lane where they had made love before he turned off onto another street, this one lined with houses. He pulled the car up to the curb in front of a modest brick ranch. Tall trees from the thick woods behind it cast the house in shadows despite the brightness of the afternoon sun.

Finally he cleared his throat and deigned to speak. "You're staying in the car."

"No." He was bigger and stronger than she was, but he wasn't going to bully her. She wasn't going to calmly accept the decisions other people made for her anymore. Her parents hadn't consulted her before dumping her on her great aunt. Jed hadn't asked if she'd wait for him before he'd dumped her. And Brandon had insisted she wear his damn ring even though she'd turned down his proposal.

People weren't going to ignore her opinions and wants and needs anymore.

"Erica, think about our daughter," he said, as if her every waking thought wasn't already about her precious baby. "She needs her mother."

"She needs her father, too," she insisted. "That's why I'm here. I have to make sure that Isobel will have the chance to get to know you."

His lips curved into a slight grin. "So you're here to protect me?"

"Yes." From himself.

"I survived three years in prison without you," he pointed out.

She shuddered at the thought of where he'd been. The things the media had reported about Blackwoods had been horrific—a warden who encouraged inmates to murder each other...

"I wouldn't have survived what you have," she admitted.

She hadn't been that strong—until she'd found herself pregnant and alone except for an aunt that had needed her help even though she hadn't been able to remember who Erica was.

She'd had to learn to be strong, so that her daughter would have someone she could count on as Erica had never been able to count on her own parents.

His smile slid away. "I don't know about that." He lifted his hand from the wheel. The blood had dried on his wound. "You're tougher than I realized."

Pride warmed her. "That's why I'm not staying in the car."

He sighed. "I guess it's better if you go inside with me than follow me in later."

As she had at the lawyer's. Then she had doubted Jed's innocence. "Do you think we'll find this man the same way we found Marcus Leighton?"

"Dead?" He nodded. "I think it's a possibility. Hopefully Rowe tracked down the man's address before the killer did." He cursed beneath his breath and muttered, "I should have come right here."

But instead he'd made love to her.

Or had he only been trying to distract her so that he could leave her behind? Neither one of them had declared any feelings for the other. But why would he fall for her now, after blaming her for his going to prison, when he hadn't fallen for her before then?

He would never love her. But maybe he would forgive her for not talking to the police when she should have. The police might have figured out what Marcus had been up to—deliberately throwing Jed's defense.

And maybe, if Erica helped prove his innocence, Isobel would forgive her, too, when one day she learned the truth about her parents. When she learned how her father had been in prison for the first few years of her life while her mother had done nothing to help him. Then.

"I'm sorry," she murmured.

"This is a bad idea," he said. "Macy shouldn't have let you stow away with me."

"Macy understood my need to help you." The young woman had acted as if Erica was in love with her brother. But Erica didn't love Jed any more than he loved her.

She had given up on love long ago—receiving it and giving it. To anyone but Isobel. Her daughter was the only one Erica would trust with her heart.

It beat faster just over Erica thinking about her. The little girl was safe with her aunt and uncle-to-be. But Jed was right that Erica wasn't safe. If she stepped inside that house with Jed, would she ever see her daughter again?

"You don't have to do this," he said. "I can drive you into town and drop you off in a well-populated area where you'll be safe until Rowe can pick you up."

"I have to do this," she corrected him.

The witness might not respond to Jed's threats, but maybe he would to her plea to give her daughter back her father. She drew in a deep, bracing breath and reached for the door handle.

Jed met her on the other side of the car. He kept glancing around as they headed toward the front door of the small brick house. "He must not have gotten as much money as Leighton."

How did one set a price for a man's life, though? Because in testifying against Jed and sending him to prison, this man had cost Jed his life.

Jed sighed. "But then he was homeless when he testified against me. This probably seems like a castle to him compared to the parking garage he was living in."

And it probably did because the yard was well kept, all the windows and trim freshly painted. There was pride in ownership. Was there pride in what he'd done to achieve the house?

If so, she would never be able to convince him to do the right thing. This man obviously felt no guilt over sending an innocent man to prison. If he had felt any remorse, he probably would have been back on the streets, lost in the bottle.

She knocked on the front door, anger making her pound so hard that the door opened.

"I don't like this," Jed remarked.

"It's broad daylight." Not like the eerie predawn hours when they had found Marcus Leighton dead in his office.

"Crime happens even during the day," he replied, reminding her how naïve she was.

Growing up in Miller's Valley with her great aunt had been like growing up in a fifty-year-old time warp. There was no crime or criminals in Miller's Valley. Everyone but her aunt had always left their doors unlocked.

That was another reason why, in addition to caring for her aunt, Erica had returned to Miller's Valley. After the fiasco with Jed and Brandon, she had wanted nothing to do with city life anymore. This house was in a smaller town, the witness having chosen to leave the city behind, too.

Jed stepped in front of her and pushed the door open the rest of the way using just his broad shoulder. Then he called out, "Hello?"

"Maybe he's gone," she said. But then she noticed the suitcase by the door.

He had intended to leave, probably after seeing the press coverage of Jed's escape from prison, but he hadn't gotten very far. The house was small and open, so it was easy to locate him without taking more than a couple of steps over the threshold. His body lay facedown by his back door, as if he had tried to make a run for it when the killer had come in his front door.

Jed crossed the living room to the kitchen and knelt beside the man, feeling his neck for a pulse. From the blood pooled on the linoleum beneath the body, Erica doubted he would find one.

He turned toward her and shook his head. "He's already cold."

"We were too late," she said. Her stomach churned with regret that they hadn't been able to save the man and that they hadn't been able to talk to him or Leighton. Or that woman who had lied about leaving Jed alone with Brandon. Had she really committed suicide, or was it murder as Jed suspected?

From the bullet hole burned through his bloodied shirt, this man had obviously been murdered. He could not tell them now who had paid him to lie on the witness stand.

Jed cursed. "We were too damn late again."

"Should we search the place?" she asked. "And try to find something linking him to whoever paid for his testimony against you?"

She was out of her element here, just as she had been from the first moment she had met Jedidiah Kleyn. But she had never been more so than now. She was a small-town bookkeeper, not a trained investigator. She had no idea how to behave at a murder scene, but at least she had managed last time and this time to control her stomach and her hysteria. She would not get sick, and she would not freak out and dissolve into sobs of hysteria.

Jed stood up. The knees of his jeans were stained with the dead man's blood. "No, we should get the hell out of here."

"But what if we miss something that could help clear you…" They couldn't help this man anymore, but maybe they could still find something that would aid Jed in his quest.

"*He* wouldn't have missed anything," Jed said, his voice rough with certainty and bitterness.

He definitely knew who had set him up. While he might not have been sure before, as he'd claimed to Rowe, he was obviously convinced now.

She glanced around, trying to discover what had cemented his conviction. But she saw nothing. "Are you sure?"

He jerked his chin down in a quick nod. "He's too smart and too thorough. The only thing he left here is a trap for me to get caught." He grabbed her hand and pulled her toward the front door.

But as he stepped toward the open doorway, shots rang out. The jamb, inches from his head, splintered. "Damnation…"

He slammed the door shut, but shots pinged against the steel and shattered the small rectangle of glass near Jed's head. Her hand still clasped in his, he pulled her along with him toward the back door. She stumbled over the body, slipping in the blood.

Jed half lifted her across the corpse and pulled open the back door. "We have to run for it," he told her as the front door creaked open, propelled either by the bullets or someone's foot.

Her heart pounded so hard, she could barely hear him. "Where do we run?"

"We can't get to the car," he said. "We'll have to run out back, into the woods."

He stepped out first onto the driveway at the side of the house, and then he pulled her out just as shots were fired inside.

Something whizzed past her head. If not for him pushing her toward the woods, she might have frozen, her muscles paralyzed with fear. But he kept her moving even as more gunfire erupted.

The backyard was wide-open with no trees or structures to deflect the bullets. He stayed between her and the house, shielding her with his body as if muscle and flesh could deflect metal.

She ran faster, her legs burning with the effort. She did not want him to take a bullet for her. And she suddenly remembered the game at the carnival where the contestant shoots the air rifle at the row of ducks.

But she wasn't the contestant with the air rifle; she was one of the ducks—waddling back and forth until the gun knocked her down.

And just a couple of yards from the woods line, she fell. She sprawled across the weeds at the edge of the lawn, her body too numb with fear for her to tell where she had been hit.

JED SPRAWLED ON TOP OF ERICA, protecting her with his body as more shots rang out behind them. More than one gun fired at them. He turned his head and peered over his shoulder.

In black uniforms with the sun glinting off the shiny badges on their chests, police officers fanned out from the house, coming toward them. But instead of identifying themselves or telling Jed and her to stop, they just kept firing.

Hoping Erica wasn't hit, Jed clutched her close. Then he rolled with her down the back slope of the lawn and into the trees. Without giving her a moment to catch her breath or for him to catch his, he dragged her up and, half carrying her, ran deeper into the woods. Briars and branches caught at his clothes and scratched his head and face.

Erica gasped and panted for breath, but she didn't slow down—just pressed close to his side as he wrapped his arm tight around her. She kept pace with him as they ran deeper and deeper into the woods. But then the crack of a shot echoed within the forest, sending birds rising up from tree branches and flying off in a frenzy. This gunshot came from ahead—not behind them.

Erica stopped short against him, realizing as he had that they were surrounded.

Trapped.

The police officers had been like deer hunters flushing out their prey to the hunter who would make the kill shot.

The killer.

Jed couldn't see him; he wasn't showing himself again—maybe because he intended to let Erica live. Or maybe because he had been in hiding for so long that he wasn't used to being out in the open.

Or he didn't want the police officers to see him. But hell, they had probably already seen him when he had paid them to help him set this trap. Maybe they didn't act out of a sense of vigilante justice but out of greed. Had they been promised more money if Jed didn't come out of these woods alive?

The officers were getting closer. Twigs and branches snapped behind him as Jed pulled Erica down into some thick brush.

She pressed her hand to her mouth, as if trying to hold back a scream or maybe just the sound of her panting breaths. She had kept pace with him through the woods, running faster than he'd thought she would be able—especially if she'd been hit when she'd first dropped to the ground at the edge of the lawn.

But then fear had probably made her oblivious to her pain and given her speed. She stared up at him, her eyes wide with questions he couldn't answer.

He didn't know how to save them. He had no gun— no weapon besides the little scalpel Macy had given Erica. Rowe wouldn't give him a gun—only the use of the vehicle and the burner cell phone.

He could call Rowe, but talking would reveal their hiding place. And Rowe would never get to them in time to save them.

Then there was no time at all for him to do anything as the cold barrel of a gun pressed into the nape of his neck.

"I'm sorry," he mouthed the words to Erica.

He would never get to know his daughter now, and he had cost the child her mother, as well. After witnessing his murder, she wouldn't be allowed to live, either.

Chapter Fifteen

"I want my mommy!" the little girl whined from her car seat in the back of the vehicle her daddy had given Macy when she'd graduated high school.

Macy glanced at the rearview mirror, but instead of checking for vehicles following them as she had constantly been doing, she met her niece's frightened gaze. Tears welled in the child's big, chocolate-brown eyes.

"I know, sweetheart," Macy commiserated with the toddler. She'd once wanted her mother, too, but Beatrice Kleyn had never been a mommy. She'd never been as loving and warm as Erica was with her daughter.

The woman had done a great job of raising her baby alone. It was obvious how much she loved Isobel. So Macy was moved that Erica had trusted her to keep the child safe. And Macy would protect her niece from all physical harm. But could she protect her from the emotional harm of losing her mommy?

Rowe had been right to get angry over her allowing Erica to stow away with Jed. She would have given up the blonde woman's whereabouts before her brother had driven off if she hadn't identified so well with the woman's need to help the man she loved.

And no matter that she hadn't been at his trial, Erica Towsley loved Jed. She'd claimed she wanted to help prove his innocence for Isobel's sake, so that her daughter would grow up knowing her father.

But Macy had seen the way Erica looked at Jed—the same way Macy looked at Rowe—like he was the only man in the world. Maybe Erica had doubted him before, and maybe she feared what he might do if he'd gone off alone to confront witnesses and track down evidence to clear himself, but she loved him.

Hopefully that love wouldn't cost Erica Towsley her life and little Isobel both her parents...

"DON'T MOVE," A DEEP raspy voice warned.

Erica couldn't have moved had she wanted to. Jed was wrapped tightly around her, once again using his own body to shield her.

But then some of the tension eased from him, and he whispered, "Rowe?"

"Shh..."

The DEA agent crouched down in the brush with them, keeping low while branches and twigs snapped around them. The taller trees blocked the late afternoon sun, casting them in shadows.

Erica held her breath but her heart pounded so hard that the sound of it echoed inside her head. Could the gunmen hear it, too? Would she be the one who gave away their location? Who cost them all their lives?

Several long moments of silence passed before Rowe's hoarse whisper advised them, "Let's go..."

Jed caught his arm and stopped him from moving from their hiding place. "The police weren't the only ones firing at us."

"You saw that guy again?"

He shook his head. "No. But he's here."

A furrow creased Rowe's brow. Then he reached be-

neath his jacket in the back and pulled out another gun.
"I didn't want to do this…"

Arm an escaped felon?

Jed hesitated before reaching for the weapon, and
then he closed his big hand around it. "Thank you."

Rowe didn't accept the gratitude, just shook his head
as if disgusted with himself. "Let's get the hell out of
here."

They backtracked through the woods. But instead of
coming up to the yard that was swarming with police
officers and crime-scene techs, they snuck through another yard several houses over that was thick with weeds
and overgrown trees, offering them cover.

The men kept her in the middle, both of them shielding her. But she caught the glint of metal as someone
raised a gun behind them. "Down!" she yelled as she
crouched low.

Bullets whizzed over their heads. But the men didn't
drop to the ground. Rowe took the lead, running toward
the street. He clicked a button on a key chain and a sliding door opened on the side of a van parked near the
curb.

Jed lifted her into the back and jumped in behind her
as Rowe slid behind the wheel. Before either door shut
completely, he was tearing away from the curb. Rubber
squealed as he careened around a corner and onto another street.

Erica's heart raced, and she trembled with nerves and
fear.

"Are you hurt?" Jed asked her. "Were you hit?"

She shook her head, realizing now that she'd only
fallen earlier because Jed had knocked her down and
knocked the breath from her lungs. She was alive, but
she was mad as hell and not just about getting shot at.

She reached into the front seat and smacked Rowe's shoulder. She didn't really care that he had rescued her and Jed. She cared only about one thing—his promise to protect her daughter. "Why did you leave her?"

"Who?" Rowe asked, sparing her only a quick glance in the rearview mirror as he continued steering the van around tight curves at high speeds.

Hysteria rose, pressing on her lungs and stealing away her breath more than the mad dash through the woods had. "Isobel! Where's Isobel?"

Jed grabbed her shoulders, as if trying to calm her down. She shook off his grasp, though, refusing to be comforted.

She had trusted Macy and Rowe to keep her daughter safe. Why, after everything she had been through in her life, had she been stupid enough to believe she could trust anyone?

"She's fine," Rowe assured her. "Don't worry about her."

"She's right to worry," Jed said, and his words offered more support than his touch. "You promised that *you* would stay with her. But you used this damn phone—" he pulled it from the pocket of her jeans; she was surprised that she hadn't lost it in the woods "—to track us."

"Macy insisted that I keep an eye on the two of you," Rowe said. "She took Isobel to safety and made me follow you to keep you safe."

"How do you know they made it to safety?" Erica asked, her panic increasing.

"Yeah, how the hell do you know?" Jed echoed her question. He apparently didn't care any more than she did that Rowe had saved his life; he cared more about their daughter's and his sister's lives.

She felt closer to him now than she had even when they had made love.

"Take us to her," she pleaded. "I have to see her." She had to hold her baby close and never let her go again.

"You can't see her now," Rowe said.

"Where did Macy take her?"

"I'm not going to tell you," he said. "It's better for her if you don't know…"

She sucked in a breath of pain. Was that what child protective services would say when they took Isobel away while the police eventually took Erica off to jail for aiding and abetting a fugitive?

"You can't go anywhere near her right now," Rowe explained, "because you would only put her in danger."

Erica posed a threat to her own daughter? Because the police were after her now or because the killer was?

"BE GOOD FOR AUNT MACY." Erica spoke into Rowe's cell phone, her voice shaky but forced into sounding bright and happy, too.

Jed already knew that she would do anything for their daughter; she was a great mother. To give Isobel her father was the reason that Erica had put her own life in jeopardy.

It was a miracle that she hadn't been hit with all the shots that had been fired at them. He shuddered now, thinking of how much danger she'd been in…because of him. Love hadn't motivated her into tagging along, though—at least not love for him. But love for their daughter…

And guilt.

"I'm glad I didn't give *her* the gun," Rowe told Jed. With an uneasy chuckle, he added, "She might have shot me back there."

"You're lucky I didn't shoot you," Jed admitted. In the heat of the moment, he hadn't realized what Erica had—that Rowe had left their daughter unprotected.

"Your sister has proven again and again that she's formidable," Rowe reminded him, with obvious pride in, and awe of, the woman he loved. "She won't let anything happen to her niece."

Jed nodded in agreement. Macy was tough—far tougher than he had ever realized. So was Erica. She had survived finding dead bodies and getting shot at, and her only worry and concern was for their child. She was another formidable woman.

"Isobel is in no danger," Rowe assured him. "She and Macy are in a safe house that only I know about, like this one."

This was a log cabin on a hill overlooking Lake Michigan. The setting sun streaked across the water and through the windows that overlooked the rocky hill that was washing away into the lake. It was a wild, beautiful, remote area just north of Muskegon.

"How the hell do you find these places?" Jed wondered. "And vehicles?" The van he'd picked them up with had been like the car, with untraceable plate and vehicle identification numbers.

"It's all seized property," the Drug Enforcement Administration agent briefly explained.

"But no one else knows about them?"

Rowe shook his head. "Not anymore. The only other agent that knew about this one and the one Macy's at is gone now."

His handler agent had recently been killed, as Rowe nearly had been in Blackwoods. While Jed regretted the agent's death, he breathed a sigh of relief. "So Macy and Isobel are really safe?"

Rowe nodded his assurance. "Yes. You and Erica aren't, though."

A headache of frustration gnawed at Jed's temples, which he rubbed. "But you said no one else living knows about this place…"

"We could have been tailed from the crime scene," Rowe said. "I don't think we were, but…"

"But this guy always seems one step ahead." At least one step. Maybe more.

"And the authorities are right behind you," Rowe needlessly reminded him.

"They never identified themselves," Jed said. "They never even tried to apprehend us. They just started shooting."

Rowe gave a grim nod. "I know. I'd like to believe that not everyone would do that, that they were convinced that you'd just killed a man and that you were armed and dangerous…"

"But you know that's not the case." They'd wanted him dead, and it had had nothing to do with protecting themselves from a dangerous suspect. It may not have had anything to do with his being convicted of killing a cop, either.

"You weren't armed," Rowe acknowledged. "Then…"

The gun was cold and heavy against the small of Jed's back. "Thanks for the weapon."

"I would rather you *not* use it."

"You and me both." But he couldn't promise that he wouldn't be forced to.

He glanced over to where Erica stood in the kitchen, leaning against the soapstone counter while she clutched the cellular in both hands, as if she was holding her daughter instead of a phone. "I need something else from you," Jed said, pitching his voice lower.

Rowe expelled a weary sigh. "I'm almost afraid to ask…"

Jed was aware and sorry that the DEA agent had had to compromise his principles and his career in order to help him. But because he had, the man deserved the truth—no matter how crazy it sounded.

"I don't think you're the only one who's faked his death," he said.

Rowe's brow furrowed with confusion. "No one thinks you're dead. You'd be a hell of a lot better off if they did, though."

"*Dead* won't clear my name," Jed pointed out, "only finding the real killer will."

"So you do know who it is…"

Jed nodded, not even caring that he might sound crazy. "He's a dead man."

"You said you weren't going to use that gun unless you had to," Rowe reminded him, with a nervous twitch of the muscle along his jaw.

"No. He's *already* a dead man," Jed clarified.

"That wasn't a dead man shooting at us," Rowe pointed out.

"He's been dead for three years," Jed explained. "At least that's what everyone believes…"

The furrows in Rowe's brow deepened as his confusion deepened. "Who the hell are you talking about?"

"Brandon Henderson, my former partner," Jed said. "The man whose murder I was sentenced to serve life in prison for."

Rowe still looked skeptical.

"Think about it," Jed said. "It all makes sense." And that was why he was disgusted with himself for not figuring it out sooner. "He embezzled the money from our clients just before I left for Afghanistan." Because Rowe had been too distracted to realize what he'd been doing. "Then he staged his murder because he knew that when I came back I would figure it out and find the money."

"I brought the books," Rowe said. "They are beyond my area of expertise."

It was Jed's area of expertise. But he hadn't thought he would have time to go over the old records, what with trying to stay ahead of the authorities determined to either put him back in prison or kill him.

"I'll go through them," Jed said. "But I can use your expertise in another area. DNA. I need you to rerun everything from the crime scene. That wasn't Brandon's body that burned up in that car."

Rowe studied his face, as if trying to gauge his sanity.

Jed waited for all the comments he had already anticipated. That he was grasping at straws. That he was crazy. Those comments and his own doubts were why he hadn't shared his suspicion with the DEA agent right away.

"You saw him?" Rowe asked.

"Not clearly," Jed admitted. "And his hair is a different color and he's wearing a beard. But my gut tells me it's him." Even though his head had kept telling him he was crazy.

After another long moment Rowe nodded. "It makes sense."

Jed should have known that if anyone would believe him, it would be the man who had already staged his own murder. In that play, Jed had also been cast as the killer.

BRANDON LIFTED HIS GUN and fired it, sending bullet after bullet into the target. He pushed a button and brought the target close to the booth at the deserted shooting range.

Jed's mug shot covered the head of the cutout. Two bullet holes pierced each of his eyes, while another single shot penetrated his forehead.

He breathed a sigh, relieved that he could have killed Jed—had he wanted. But it had been more satisfying to have the man trapped in the brush like a rabbit—too stupid and helpless to save himself or the woman he loved.

The officers Brandon paid had come through for him, shooting *at* but not hitting Jed. Just as they had been instructed. He hadn't even had to pay them much since they thought Jed a cop killer and Brandon a relative of the deceased officer who wanted justice. They had been more than happy to help him.

He had thought that, given his convictions, Jed would have had no one to help him. But someone had come to his rescue, getting him out of the woods and into a getaway vehicle before Brandon could kill him. First he would have killed Erica Towsley, though.

The stupid prude hadn't given him the time of day, but she had given Jed everything. Her heart. Her soul. Even a child.

When he killed the woman and the little girl, he would take all those things away from Jed. Then—and only then, when the man had absolutely nothing—would Brandon take his *best* friend's life.

He didn't even have to try to track down Jed again. Brandon knew him too well. Jed would find *him* this time. And when Jed did, Brandon would be waiting… and ready.

He lifted his gun and fired again.

And again.

Brandon pushed the button and brought his target back to the booth. The face of the outline had been covered with a picture he had taken from the collection of family photos in Erica Towsley's apartment. It was the gorgeous blonde, smiling brightly, as she held her daughter tight in her arms.

A bullet hole pierced the paper between her beautiful blue eyes. A matching hole pierced the paper between the big, dark eyes of the child.

He would definitely be ready next time to, once and for all, win this rivalry with Jedidiah Kleyn.

Chapter Sixteen

A fire burned inside the hearth, the flames casting light and warmth on Erica. She stood in front of it, but she couldn't stop shivering.

It was the conversation she had overheard before the DEA had left, not the cold, that had chilled her to the bone. The outside door creaked open, so she reached into her pocket and closed her fingers around the sheathed scalpel. Jed had gone outside to say goodbye to his friend and future brother-in-law, but that didn't mean he was the one coming back inside. She'd heard an engine a while ago and had just assumed it was from the car Rowe had had stashed in the garage. But what if it had been that other car, the one that had nearly forced them off the road leading away from Miller's Valley? What if they had been followed from the house of the dead witness?

Something crashed, and she withdrew her weapon and whirled around. Jed stood next to the box he had dropped onto the rough-hewn wood coffee table.

"Sorry," he said. "I didn't mean to scare you."

A laugh, more from hysteria than mirth, bubbled out of her. "Not this time," she conceded. "But you've wanted to scare me other times. Like when you first showed up at my door."

"I wanted to scare you into doing the right thing then," he said.

"Coming forward as your alibi."

"Instead I scared you into doing the wrong thing," Jed remarked with a weary-sounding sigh. He dropped onto the floor next to the coffee table and lifted the lid from the banker's box.

"Wrong thing?" she questioned. What had she done wrong besides trusting her daughter to a relative stranger? Besides nearly losing her life? Apparently she'd done everything wrong.

"I made you feel guilty, and now you've risked your life to help me prove my innocence," he said, his eyes dark with regret and torment. "I never wanted that. I never wanted to put you in any danger."

She laughed again with more dark humor than hysteria now. "I imagine, since you believed I helped set you up, you spent the past three years wanting to kill me yourself."

His mouth curved into a slight grin. "Maybe," he conceded.

"I don't blame you," she said. "I can't imagine being locked up for crimes I didn't commit."

"You believe that now?" he asked. "Because I still see doubts in your eyes." But he wasn't looking at her. He was focused on the contents of the box instead.

She nodded and admitted, "I have doubts." About the kind of man he had become, about what he was capable of. And now she had something else to doubt. "I overheard what you told Rowe."

His broad shoulders tensed, but he didn't look up from the files he'd pulled from the box. "You did?"

She shuddered. "It's not possible. Brandon Henderson can't be alive."

"It's possible to fake your own death," Jed said. "Rowe did it when his cover was blown in Blackwoods, and we had a lot less time to plan his escape than Brandon had to plan his."

"Escape?" she repeated. "What would Brandon need to escape from?" The man had loved his life and lived it to the fullest, going to the nicest restaurants, owning the fastest cars and wearing the most expensive tailored suits.

"Embezzlement charges," Jed replied. "When I was deployed for that year, he must have started embezzling from our clients."

She nodded with sudden understanding of Brandon's motive. "And he would know that you would figure out what he had done when you returned. And that you would turn him in."

Jedidiah Kleyn had been the kind of man who would always do the right thing. Was he still that kind of man?

"I think he was counting on me not coming back," Jed said.

She gasped. "He didn't think you would make it home from Afghanistan?"

She hadn't been the only one to think that he was never coming back. But then, in her experience, people didn't come back for her once they'd left her...

Jed nodded. "That was probably when he decided to start siphoning money from my clients' accounts."

"Because he had a scapegoat for the embezzlement charges that would eventually be filed when the clients discovered their money missing," she said, following how Brandon's twisted mind would have worked. "But how could he frame you when you were gone..."

She joined him at the table, stepping away from the

fire; it wasn't warming her. "How could he make it look like you were responsible?"

"Because he started when I got my orders—when I was still home but distracted." He glanced up at her, as if she were to blame for his being distracted. But he had broken up with her.

He hadn't even given her the chance to find the courage to wait for him. If he'd given her any indication that he'd shared her feelings, she might have become brave...

He returned his attention to one of the files. "And he was tapping my clients, the accounts that I thought I was the only one who could access."

"Are you sure it was him?" she asked.

"You think it was me again?" he asked, his voice gruff with frustration. "You think I embezzled that money but hired Marcus as my lawyer? I knew he wasn't the most competent representation, but he was a friend. He was also all I could afford."

In the end, Marcus Leighton had cost him much more than money, though. He had cost Jed his reputation and three years of his life and maybe more if they couldn't find any evidence to clear him.

She knelt on the floor beside him and reached for the files. "Can I help?"

"You've already done more than you should have," Jed said. "I shouldn't involve you anymore."

"It's too late." She had been too involved even before he'd broken out of prison and shown up at her door flashing a DEA badge.

As she knelt beside him, he reached out and grabbed her hand. "I'm sorry. I'll do everything I can so no charges are pressed against you for aiding and abetting. I don't know if anyone will believe me, but I'll swear that I coerced you, that I threatened you."

"It's my own fault," she admitted although she was touched that he would try to take the blame and risk more charges against him. "I shouldn't have insisted on going along with you to Leighton's. I shouldn't have stowed away in the car at the hangar."

"Why did you?"

"For Isobel," she assured him, so that he didn't worry that she was falling for him. It was enough that she worry. "She deserves to have a father."

"I'm not sure how this will all turn out," he cautioned her. "Even if I'm cleared of the murder charges, I will face other charges for breaking out of prison."

"So, no matter what, you're going to have to go back?" She should have realized as much, but she'd just been focused on learning the truth of what had happened three years ago. She hadn't thought about current charges. So no matter what, Isobel would be denied a relationship with her father.

Disappointment overwhelmed Erica, and she realized she wasn't upset just for her daughter. But she didn't want a relationship with Jed, though.

He had already broken her heart more than once; she knew better than to ever risk it on him again. Especially now, knowing that he wouldn't truly be free even if he was cleared of the murder charges.

"I don't know how long they'll give me for breaking out," he said. "It won't be as long as a murder sentence. I will get out again."

"That'll only happen if you're still alive," she said. And if Brandon was alive, if he stayed alive and Jed didn't kill him when he caught up with him. Or Jed would wind up serving time for murder. Even if he didn't kill Brandon, he might be charged with killing his lawyer and the other witness. It didn't matter that he was innocent; a case could still be made against him, just as it had in the murders of Brandon and the police officer.

"I survived three years in Blackwoods—"

"Back at the witness's house those cops were all shooting at you." And her. But she couldn't remember that or she would start trembling in reaction. She had held it together during their ordeal, but exhaustion undermined the strength she hadn't known she had.

"That's because they think I'm a cop killer," he said. "That's why I need to prove it wasn't me."

"It was Brandon?"

"You don't think he's alive?" he asked, studying her face again as if trying to gauge if she thought he was crazy for even considering it.

She shrugged. "I don't know what to believe about anything anymore." She had spent the past three years believing an innocent man guilty. She could have also spent three years believing a live man dead.

"Help me find proof then," he said, and he passed her a file folder.

After going through that one, she grabbed another and another. Reading through printed ledgers and bank statements, her eyelids drooped, growing almost too heavy to keep open. Maybe if she closed them for just a moment...

She jerked awake, disoriented from a sense of weightlessness and moving, almost as if she were flying, through a dark room. She opened her lips to utter the scream choking her.

"It's okay," Jed assured her. "I'm bringing you to bed."

Her pulse quickened and then raced.

"You're exhausted," he said.

"But I didn't find anything to help you. I need to keep looking over the statements," she protested, struggling in his arms.

He lowered her to a soft mattress. "You're not going to find anything. The son of a bitch covered his tracks very well. The transfers from my client accounts all went into my account."

"But the money isn't there anymore."

"It sure as hell isn't," he replied with a bitter chuckle. "There was a transfer to an untraceable, offshore account."

Purpose reinvigorated her, chasing away her drowsiness. "We need to find that bank and get proof that the account belongs to Brandon."

Jed shook his head. "Those banks constantly change their routing and transit numbers to hide their assets as well as their clients' assets. We're not going to track them down."

"And we're not going to track down Brandon." She shivered. "He's going to track down us."

Rowe's safe house wouldn't stay safe long—not if Brandon was really still alive and hell-bent on protecting himself. He had already fired at them in the woods. What would he do to them here?

"I won't let him hurt you," Jed promised. "I'll protect you." He stepped back, but before he could turn toward the door, she reached for him.

She clutched his hand. "Who will protect me from you?" she asked because Erica was afraid that she was going to fall for him again, and he had already broken her heart too many times.

He shook his head. "I'm sorry about earlier—about taking advantage of you..."

"I'm not," she admitted. "And you didn't take advantage of me."

He had given her the chance to change her mind, but she'd wanted him too much. Then. And now.

She tugged him down onto the bed with her.

"Erica, this is a bad idea," he warned her. "I told you that I'll have to go back to jail. We have no future."

"I know," she assured him. And maybe that was why she wanted to make love with him so badly—because she didn't know if she would ever be this close to him again. She didn't have to worry about her heart; she didn't have to worry if she should trust him.

She only had to worry about holding on to her heart tonight.

"You deserve more," he said.

"I have more," she assured him. "I have Isobel." Their daughter was all she needed in her life.

The little girl was safe; Macy had assured her of that earlier. And she had believed it when she'd talked to Isobel. While the little girl had missed her mommy, she had also been thrilled to be getting to know her fun, new aunt.

If only Isobel would be able to get to know her father, too...

But Jed was right; there hadn't been any clues left in those ledgers and bank statements. Nothing to clear his name, nothing to point to Brandon's guilt or his present whereabouts if he really wasn't six feet under.

Jed expelled a ragged breath. "You are so beautiful," he murmured, "whenever you talk about our daughter, you glow...like an angel..."

She didn't feel like an angel tonight. She reached for the bottom of her sweater and dragged it up and over her head. She tossed it onto the floor, and then she unclasped her bra.

Jed groaned now. "Damn, woman…"

He followed her lead but shucked off all his clothes and then dragged her jeans down her legs. He kissed her everywhere, taking his time first with her mouth. He pressed hot kisses to her lips and then parted them for his tongue. He kissed her deeply.

She arched against him and moaned, wanting all of him. Pressure built inside her, making her ache for him. But he was pulling back to kiss her shoulders, the inside of her elbow, the curve of her hip. He dipped his tongue inside her navel and then moved it lower. She lifted off the bed. "Jed!"

He made love to her thoroughly until tears streaked from her eyes as the pressure wound tighter, then released in a rush of pleasure. "Jed!"

He parted her legs and thrust inside, joining their bodies as their hearts would never be joined. Except that, as she clutched him close, she felt his heart beating in perfect, frantic rhythm with hers. It was as if they shared one heart, one body.

He kissed her passionately, as he thrust deep inside her. She arched and clutched at him, digging her nails into his back and then lower, into his butt.

He groaned. "I can't—" His control snapped and he came, filling her.

And she joined him, her scream of ecstasy echoing his shout. She didn't let go, didn't let him go, but fell asleep holding him close…until she wouldn't be able to hold him anymore…

A RINGING NOISE JERKED Jed awake. He hadn't heard a phone ring in three years, but he recognized the sound and fumbled for the phone that lay atop his jeans beside the bed. He glanced at the woman lying beside him. Maybe she slept as soundly as their daughter because she didn't so much as shift or murmur over the noise or his moving beside her.

He had to pull his arm out from under her. It tingled, asleep even from her slight weight. He slipped out of bed and took the phone with him out to the living room. Studying the high-tech screen on the cellular, he pushed a button but didn't say anything.

"Jed?"

He grunted as he recognized Rowe's voice. "Yeah…"

"Sounds like I woke you up," the DEA agent mused. "I didn't think you would be able to sleep."

If not for making love with Erica, he wouldn't have been able to close his eyes…not without the fear of seeing Brandon's face.

"I haven't slept since I broke out," he admitted. "Actually not since the riot started."

"Guess you haven't had a safe place to sleep until tonight," Rowe remarked.

"I have to wonder how safe any place is," Jed said. "It's him, isn't it?"

"Yes!" Rowe said with triumph. "I had an FBI tech rush the DNA report from the old crime-scene evidence. We got what we need to get a new trial, Jed!"

"I don't want a new trial," he said. "I want justice. He's not dead?" Yet.

"It wasn't Brandon Henderson in the burned-out vehicle," Rowe confirmed. "The dental records used at the trial were obviously fakes."

"Why wasn't DNA used then?" Jed wondered.

"It was ordered but the results weren't back before the trial," Rowe said. "And your lawyer agreed with the

D.A. that the dental records were confirmation enough of the dead body's identity."

Jed cursed Marcus and himself for so blindly trusting him. Hell, he'd trusted Brandon, too—not much but enough to go into business with the man. Brandon Henderson had been smart and ambitious; Jed had had no doubt that theirs would be a successful firm.

He just hadn't realized exactly how smart and ambitious Brandon was.

And how criminal…

"You could have had a new trial at any time," Rowe said, the triumph replaced with the hard edge of anger, "if anyone had bothered to follow up about the DNA."

"I don't want a new trial," Jed repeated.

"But just because Brandon wasn't in the car doesn't make him the killer."

"Bullshit," Jed replied, his frustration growing. "If he wasn't the killer, why hasn't he come forward before now?"

"He came forward in the woods today," Rowe said. "There were shells found from a gun that wasn't police issue."

"So shouldn't that help clear me or at least get the shoot-on-sight order rescinded?"

Rowe cursed now. "Those unidentified shells prove to the police that you're armed and dangerous because they think that gun was yours. I have to bring you in, Jed. Or you'll get shot for sure. But until we can get that new trial, the DNA evidence will be enough to cast doubt on your convictions. You'll be safer now."

"No." He wouldn't be safe until Brandon was six feet under for real. The man had gone to a lot of trouble to take away from Jed everything that had mattered to him—his reputation, his freedom.

Erica…

He glanced toward the bedroom and jumped when he noticed her leaning against the doorjamb. She was wearing his shirt with only half the buttons done up, displaying her slender legs and the hollow between her full breasts. His body hardened again, wanting her.

Rowe was still talking. "I'm not giving you a choice, man. I'm going to be back there in a couple of hours, and I'm bringing you in."

"No," Jed repeated. Instead of arguing with him, he just clicked off the cell. He wouldn't be there by the time Rowe arrived.

"No?" Erica asked. "It wasn't him?"

"It wasn't him in the car," Jed confirmed.

She sucked in a sharp breath of air and fear. "So Brandon's still alive?"

He nodded. *For now.*

"Do you know where he is?" she asked.

He forced a shrug. But he knew. Brandon was waiting for him. Just like Jed, he would have realized that it was time for them to end this. Their rivalry had begun in elementary school and had lasted too damn long. Jed had always considered it a healthy, competitive rivalry that had made them both stronger and more successful.

That hadn't been the case. It hadn't been healthy for either of them, or for anyone who had come into contact with them. Erica had been hurt. Marcus Leighton and the witnesses were all dead…

"You know where he is," Erica said, with that insight into him that no one but Macy had ever had. "And you intend to kill him."

He had to kill Brandon before the man killed him. Or worse yet—her and Isobel.

Despite the late hour, the jail was alive—excitement dancing in the air and in Jefferson's lawyer's eyes. Something had happened.

Hopefully something good for him.

"Looks like the DEA agent may have been right about Kleyn," Breuker remarked. He drummed his fingers against his briefcase. "A source informed me that the agent rushed DNA from the old crime scene."

"It wasn't Kleyn's?"

"It wasn't the man he was accused of killing—his business partner."

He choked out a laugh at the irony. "He faked his death…" Like Kleyn had talked an undercover agent into faking his to save his life.

But this wasn't good news for Jefferson. Having an innocent man testify against him would be so much worse than having a convicted killer…

"This is bad news," he pointed out, wondering at his lawyer's excitement. Maybe the man wasn't as brilliant as his reputation claimed, just as Jed Kleyn hadn't been as ruthless as his.

"York and Ketchum are having a big powwow right now," Breuker shared. "Something's going down…"

"A showdown," Jefferson mused.

Kleyn might have been an innocent man when he'd been sentenced to Blackwoods, but three years there had stolen away that innocence and his humanity.

"He's going to want revenge."

"And his partner's going to want to protect himself…"

Jefferson laughed again as the lawyer's excitement

tingled in his veins. "Sounds like they might wind up killing each other..."

And that would be very good news for Jefferson James.

Chapter Seventeen

Erica shivered at the coldness on Jed's handsome face. He hadn't denied her accusation. He fully intended to kill Brandon Henderson.

She had been right not to give him her heart. He wasn't the man she had once known and loved. Maybe Afghanistan hadn't changed him, but Brandon's betrayal and Blackwoods Penitentiary had.

"How can you just kill a man in cold blood?" she asked, horrified.

He laughed. "You think it'll be in cold blood? I think it'll be in self-defense."

Erica shook her head, denying his claim. "No. You know where he is. You don't have to go there to meet him. Call Rowe back. Tell him where he can find Brandon. He'll bring him in alive."

"He won't know if it's Brandon or not. The guy's changed his appearance," Jed reminded her. "Rowe won't recognize him from some old photograph."

He was probably right; Brandon was too smart to waltz back into the country looking like his old, *dead* self. "Then go with Rowe. Point Brandon out, but stay out of it."

"Brandon took away three years of my life. He broke into your house, probably to abduct our daughter, and then he shot at us," he said, listing the man's recent crimes. "I'm not giving him the chance to take anything else away from me."

She laughed now, just as he had, with irony and bitterness. "If you kill him, he'll take away your humanity and your honor."

"He took that away when I got locked up in hell three years ago."

Yes. Blackwoods had changed him.

"I'm going with you," she insisted, turning for the bedroom to grab her clothes.

Jed followed her in and grabbed up his clothes, too. He pulled on his jeans and shirt and then lifted the gun from the floor.

God, why had Rowe given him a gun?

"You're not going with me," he said. He didn't point the gun at her, but there was something threatening about just the way he held it, staring down at the trigger as if he could pull it with his gaze since his finger was nowhere near it.

"You're not going to shoot me," she said, calling his unspoken bluff.

"Why not?" he asked. "According to you, I'm a cold-blooded killer." He stared at her now instead of at the gun, but his dark eyes weren't cold. They were full of emotion—anger and hurt.

"Not yet," she said. "But if you confront Brandon alone, you're going to become one."

"You're not coming along," he insisted. "I don't want you anywhere near Brandon ever again."

The man had tried to use her before to hurt Jed; he would undoubtedly have no qualms about using her again. "I don't want to be anywhere near him," she admitted. "And I don't want you near him, either. I want you to wait for Rowe."

He shook his head. "I can't. I've waited three years for justice, Erica. I can't wait any longer." He shoved the gun into the waistband of his jeans at his back as he turned for the door.

She reached for his arm, trying to hold him back. Muscles bulged and rippled beneath her grasp, and he gently shook her off. But he stopped in the doorway and faced her again.

Maybe she'd gotten through to him. Maybe he'd changed his mind about meeting Brandon alone. She breathed a slight sigh of relief.

Then he stole her breath with a kiss. It was deep and full of passion and promise. She closed her eyes and smiled, grateful that he had changed his mind.

For her?

Did he want to be the man she had once fallen for, the man she had once loved?

He lifted his mouth from hers and stepped back because she couldn't feel the heat of his body anymore.

"Jed…" She opened her eyes. But she didn't see his face. She only saw wood as the door snapped shut between them. She reached for the knob, grabbing it, but it wouldn't budge.

He was either holding it, or he must have shoved something beneath it, because moments later an engine revved.

Tears stung her eyes. "Damn you, Jed…"

He might have had to go back to prison because of the escape. But he wouldn't have had to serve much time—not what he would have to serve for murder.

Isobel would never get to know her father. And Erica would be left with only a few memories of her passionate lover. He would never be anything more to her, never be part of her future—only a bittersweet part of her past.

No. They all deserved more than that; they all deserved a future. He might have jammed the door, but he hadn't had time to lock the window. She crossed the room to it and lifted the sash. The ground dropped off below, moonlight shimmering on the rocky hillside. If she tried going out that way, Brandon Henderson might not be the only one who died tonight...

SOMEONE WAS GOING to die tonight.

Unlike Erica, Jed wasn't as convinced that he could pull the trigger and take a life. He had the reasons and the rage to want to. It wouldn't be in cold blood, as Erica had said, that he would kill. It would be in hot blood.

Anger heated his body, so that he didn't notice the cold wind blowing around as he walked down the ramp leading to the basement of the parking garage. This was where he would find Brandon and where he should kill him—since this was the crime scene where he had already been convicted of killing him.

No attendant sat inside the booth. The gates stayed down, so Jed skirted around them. The security lights had been broken out; glass crunched beneath his feet as he strode through the darkness. But moonlight crept over the concrete walls, casting an eerie glow on the cement and shifting the shadows of the few cars parked inside the garage.

"You took your time," a deep voice remarked. "And you're already a man on borrowed time."

His gut tightened with dread. He didn't need to see Brandon's half-assed disguised face. His voice was unmistakable—not just the tone and the timbre of it but the arrogance in it. Nobody else was that damn cocky.

It used to amuse Jed; now it infuriated him…because Brandon was entitled to that arrogance. He had fooled everyone.

Even Jed.

"I've got all the time in the world," he said with a bitter laugh. "You saw to that."

"Two lifetimes." Brandon's perfectly capped teeth flashed brightly in the shadows. "But you're taking a little break right now. It won't last, you know, not with all those cops out looking for you." He laughed. "If they find you, you won't last long at all."

Jed yawned as if bored with Brandon. The man had always prided himself on being everything but boring. "That's old news now. I'm old news. The hot new story is how you faked your own death."

"Good luck proving that."

"DNA came back." Probably years ago. "It proves that yours wasn't the body in the car."

Brandon snorted, dismissing the evidence. "That doesn't prove that I'm alive and well."

"Oh, you're not well at all," Jed agreed. "You're batshit crazy, my old friend."

Brandon laughed again but with genuine humor this time. "I have missed you, my old friend," he said, turning Jed's words back on him. "You always entertained me."

"I always annoyed the hell out of you," Jed corrected him, "because you could never be better than me."

Brandon's voice rose with patronization as he replied, "I think we both know that's not the case anymore."

The son of a bitch was choosing his words carefully,

as he always had. He had always managed just enough charm to hide the fact that he was actually a psychopath.

"You ruined my life," Jed admitted. "But I'm thinking you ruined your own life, too."

"How's that?"

"You're not *you* anymore," he scoffed. He wasn't talking about the blond dye or the colored contacts and the unkempt goatee, although those were all things macho Brandon Henderson would have mocked.

"Fishing for my new name?" Brandon laughed at his attempt. "Fish away…"

"Your name meant something to you," Jed reminded him, striking out at the only place Brandon felt anything—his pride. "You wanted everyone to know it. But no one remembers the first murder victim from my trial. They remember the officer who died too young in the line of duty."

Brandon snorted. "Line of duty or wrong place at the wrong time?"

"I guess only the young officer himself would know that, and of course, the man who really killed him would know…"

"I guess," Brandon conceded without really conceding anything at all.

"But the thing people remember most from my trial is *me*. It's *my* name everyone remembers," Jed taunted him. "It's *me* everyone talks about." And he'd hated that so much. But Brandon wouldn't understand that; he'd never cared about what people said about him as long as he was all they talked about…

Brandon's wide shoulders moved in the shadows in a jerky shrug—his nonchalance totally feigned. His pride was stinging as well as that resentment of Jed that he'd never quite been able to hide or control. He struck back at Jed with, "That must drive you crazy—that everyone talks about how the hero became a villain."

"At least they're talking about *me*. You're entirely forgotten, my friend. I think even you have forgotten who you are." He tsked his tongue against the roof of his mouth, pouring on the pity.

"I know who I am," Brandon insisted. "You're the one who's lost himself. You've totally changed."

"Yes. I have," Jed conceded. "I wasn't a killer when you framed me for your murder and that young officer's murder."

Brandon snorted again. "But you are a killer now?"

Jed lifted his gun. "I will be."

"You want a third life sentence?"

"I can't be convicted of your murder again," Jed reminded him. "That would be double jeopardy." He moved his finger to the trigger and prepared to squeeze.

"No!" a female voice screamed. Panting for breath, Erica ran into the parking garage as if she'd run all the way from the lake. "Don't do it, Jed. Don't kill him."

"Damn it! Get out of here!" he yelled at her. His heart hammered against his ribs. Even knowing what a monster Brandon really was, he hadn't been afraid for himself.

But Erica...

Before she could run back the way she'd run in, Brandon grabbed her. He locked his arm around her torso, trapping her arms against her sides, and then he pressed a gun to her temple.

Erica's eyes widened with fear. She hadn't thought her action through—hadn't realized the danger she was putting herself in...

Jed had known the man would be armed and ready and that he would be waiting for just this opportunity.

Brandon wanted to kill Jed but not before he made him suffer more.

"Don't hurt her," he pleaded.

"You're the one who keeps hurting her," Brandon said. "You dumped her before you left for Afghanistan."

"I didn't want to do that," Jed said. "But I didn't want her waiting for me."

"Yeah, you were being self-sacrificing and heroic," Brandon said with heavy disgust.

"I was scared," Jed admitted. "I didn't think I was coming home."

Brandon sighed. "Yes, I thought you were going to die over there, too."

"That's why you started embezzling from my accounts." He wasn't just trying to get him talking now; he was trying to figure out how to distract him so that he could get Erica out of danger.

Brandon glanced around the parking garage, as if looking for witnesses. Maybe the police officer would have still been alive if Brandon had done that the last time he'd been in this garage.

"Come on," Jed said. "You're going to kill her. I'm going to kill you. Before you go down, you may get a shot off that eventually kills me. Don't you think I deserve to know the truth before I die?"

Brandon chuckled. "That must have been the worst thing about your three years in prison—not knowing who put you there or why."

"Was it because of me?" Erica asked, her voice trembling with fear. "Did you want to put Jed away because you wanted me?"

Brandon laughed heartily now. "You think I was in love with you?"

The man was a narcissist; he loved no one but himself. That was why his former girlfriend and witness for the prosecution was dead; he hadn't needed her. He hadn't ever needed anyone. If only Jed had realized that before he'd agreed to become the man's business partner...

"I was just using you to get to him," Brandon admitted.

"Like now," Jed said.

"But I wouldn't marry you. I only went out with you to feel close to Jed," she said, "so we could talk about him."

Brandon groaned. "I know. Everything's always been about Jed. All my life. My parents were so damn impressed with him. Our teachers. Our clients. Everything was about brilliant, honorable Jedidiah Kleyn."

"So you weren't in love with me," she said, "you were in hate with Jed."

"To frame me for murder—your murder—and send me to prison, you really have to hate me," Jed said.

"Hate is too mild a word for what I feel for you, my old friend," Brandon admitted, the words surging forth as his control finally snapped. "I thought it would be enough to destroy your reputation, to send you to prison, but it's not..."

"What about the money?" Jed asked. "Hasn't that made you happy? You embezzled nearly a million dollars from my clients."

Brandon shrugged, his grip loosening slightly around Erica. Instead of taking advantage, though, and struggling, she stood perfectly still, as if hoping the man would forget all about her. Maybe, with his focus so completely on Jed, he would.

"It was more than a million," Brandon boasted. "And I've doubled that since. I'm a very wealthy man."

"Isn't that enough?" Jed asked. "I'm in prison and you're rich."

"You weren't supposed to last in prison," Brandon said, "just like you weren't supposed to last in Afghanistan."

"You wanted me dead so that I wouldn't eventually figure it out," Jed realized.

"I wanted you dead so I didn't have to keep hearing about you," Brandon said, nearly gagging on the admission as if just the thought of Jed made him physically sick.

"You stayed around here?" Jed asked.

"No, but I stayed in touch with Marcus, making sure that no new evidence came up that would get you off on an appeal."

"That had to be expensive," Jed mused. "Marcus was always very nervous. You would have had to keep paying him to keep him quiet. Is that why you finally killed him?"

"I should have killed him years ago," Brandon admitted.

"Like you killed the woman?"

His bright teeth flashed again. "That was a suicide."

"It was murder. And if you'd killed Leighton, the authorities might have figured out it was strange that everyone from my trial was dying."

"Especially while you were prison," Brandon agreed.

"So you would have had no one to blame for Marcus's murder. Or the other witness's."

Brandon's teeth flashed in another grin. "You breaking out of prison really helped me tie up the loose ends I had to leave after the last murders."

"And what about me and Erica now?" Jed asked. "What are we?"

Brandon shrugged. "Just more loose ends…"

Jed had never hated the man more than he did right now. How could he dismiss Erica Towsley—who was a loving, devoted mother—as nothing more than a loose end?

If only Jed could get the shot…

But even though Brandon had loosened his grip around Erica, he still held the gun pressed against her temple with his finger right on the trigger. If Jed took the shot and missed, she was dead. If Jed took the shot and hit him, she might still be dead; Brandon could pull the trigger as a reflex before he died.

JED WAS DYING TO KILL HIM. Brandon could see the hatred in his eyes as he studied his options, trying to determine if he dared to take a shot.

He wasn't the man Brandon was. He wouldn't dare. He cared too much about the woman to risk her life. So, soon Jed would just be dying.

All these years of anticipation and it might be over this quick? Brandon wanted to savor the moment, wanted to taunt him a little bit more. He leaned forward and pressed his face into the woman's hair.

Erica shuddered as if in revulsion.

"Oh, come on, honey," he said. "Don't act like you don't like it when I touch you. You went out with me after this guy dumped you. You wanted to see what a real man was all about."

Jed's darkly stubbled jaw tensed, a muscle twitching in his cheek.

"If only I had time to show you now," Brandon teased. "You would forget all about this guy—just like you did before. But I don't have time."

He had a private plane to catch, to bring him back to

the island with no extradition treaty where he had spent most of the past three years. He hadn't trusted Marcus or the witness not to eventually give him up.

But when he'd heard about Jed's escape, he'd had to return. The opportunity had been too good to pass up.

Brandon figured either Jed or the woman had some kind of recorder, taping his confession. That was why Jed had kept him talking instead of just killing him the minute he had stepped into the parking garage.

If Jed had stolen three years of his life, his money and his reputation, Brandon would have killed him the minute he'd seen him. Jed cared more about honor than revenge. His very integrity would be what finally destroyed him completely, though.

Brandon would just kill them both and check them for recording devices, probably Jed was using the voice recorder on his cell phone. Brandon would destroy that and then no one would ever know the truth.

"I really appreciate you making this easy for me," he told them. "Your showing up here, Erica, makes it all so easy to stage another double murder. Or should I say murder, suicide."

He grinned as his new plan took shape and taunted them with the details. "Jed here is going to kill himself before going back to prison, and because he doesn't want any other man to have you, he's going to kill you, Erica, before he takes his own life…in the very same spot where he committed those murders three years ago."

"Who was he?" Jed asked.

He snapped at the inane interruption. "Who?"

"The man you passed off as yourself," Jed reminded him. "The man you murdered and then burned his body to pass off as yours."

Brandon sighed. "Enough with the questions. It doesn't matter anymore. You're not going to prove your innocence. And you're not going to stall me until help arrives." He laughed at his own joke. "Help? You have no one who can help you."

He must have just imagined that Jed'd had help to escape the woods because if he'd had someone there, the guy would have been here already. He wouldn't have let him walk into the parking garage alone, and he certainly wouldn't have let Erica run between two armed men—especially if it was the DEA agent, the only person besides Jed's sister who had expressed belief in his innocence.

"Everybody hates you now," he reminded Jed. "Your parents, your clients—everyone who thought you were such a hero has forsaken you. Even you…" He pressed a kiss to Erica's temple where he didn't hold the gun. "You doubted him. You believed he was a killer."

"I didn't… I wouldn't have…" she stammered, "but Marcus convinced me."

He snorted in derision. "Marcus never made a compelling argument in his life. You doubted Jed because you didn't trust him then. And you don't trust him now or you wouldn't have shown up here. So I guess you really have no one, Jed, not even the woman you love…"

He cocked the gun. It was time to pull the trigger— time to end all this nonsense and get back to paradise.

Chapter Eighteen

"You've been so brave," Macy praised her niece, keeping her voice bright and happy.

Over the phone, Erica had calmed her daughter's fears but for just a short while. The little girl must have felt the same awful sense of foreboding that gripped Macy. Something bad was going to happen.

Lives were going to be lost—futures destroyed.

And Macy was helpless to do anything to prevent the pending tragedy. She had accepted her role in this horrible play when she'd promised Erica to keep the little girl safe. As she pulled her car up outside the parking garage, she realized that Erica probably wouldn't consider this the best way to protect the child.

She wasn't bringing her into the line of fire. But they would be able to hear shots from here. They'd be able to know when it was over...just not whose lives were over...

CHOKING ON FEAR, ERICA HELD her breath. It wasn't supposed to go like this, but then nothing had gone according to her plan since she had first met Jedidiah Kleyn. She'd been applying for a job and wound up with a boyfriend. But she hadn't kept him.

She had already known that she wouldn't be able to

keep him now. But she hadn't suspected that she was the one who might wind up dead. Of course it should have occurred to her, since she'd run out between two men holding guns on each other.

But still...it wasn't supposed to go like this.

The look on Jed's face would haunt her...for however long she lived. Fear and horror darkened his eyes even more, so that they looked more black than brown.

"I'm sorry." She mouthed the words to him as he'd once mouthed them to her. And she flinched, waiting for the bullet to strike. That little scalpel she carried wouldn't protect her now. Before she could unsheathe it and stab Brandon, she would be dead.

"You're wrong," Jed told Brandon.

The guy laughed. "This should be good. What am I wrong about? Are you going to try to save her? Going to try to hit me? Your bullet won't be able to hit me before mine tears her brain apart."

Erica shivered at the coldness of Brandon's voice. She had once been taken in by his charm. Not enough to fall for him but enough to go out with him even though she had already been in love with another man.

"You're wrong that I have no friends," Jed informed him. "That I have no one to help me."

Brandon lifted the gun slightly away from her head and glanced around. "I don't see anyone else here. It's just the three of us. For the moment."

"You're not looking hard enough," Jed advised him. "Look harder..."

"We're right here," a raspy voice added, and Rowe stepped from the shadows behind Brandon, his gun trained on the madman's head.

"And if Kleyn and Cusack aren't able to get off a shot

fast enough to save Ms. Towsley, I sure as hell will," added another male voice.

Erica glanced up to where Sheriff York stood on the parking level above them, a sniper rifle trained on Brandon's forehead. And if he doubted the man, he would only have to look in a mirror to see the red laser mark between his eyes.

Brandon sucked in a breath of shock and fear.

"It's over," Jed informed him. "They heard everything."

"And we had the D.A.'s approval to record it," the sheriff added. "In fact he's been listening in the entire time…"

Brandon's breath escaped in a gasp and a curse. "Son of a bitch…"

Erica didn't relax. It might be over according to Jed and the lawmen. But Brandon was used to calling the shots. He was used to having things go his way. He wasn't likely to go out how these men wanted him—in handcuffs—but in a blaze of glory. And he would take her with him, caught in the crossfire.

She saw that same fear in Jed's eyes as he waited, his gun still trained on Brandon.

They might all die yet.

But then Brandon lowered his weapon and stepped back. Obviously he hadn't wanted to die for real. "Goddamn you, Jed. I thought I'd taken you down. Finally. I'd thought you lost."

"If it makes you feel any better," Jed told him as Rowe slapped cuffs around the man's wrists, "you took away three years of my life that I'll never get back. Three years of time I could have spent with my daughter."

Three years of time he could have spent with her.

Erica wanted to tell him that, but he wasn't looking at her. Until Rowe led Brandon away, reading him his rights. Then Jed walked up and grabbed her, shaking her gently.

"What the hell were you thinking, woman?" he asked, his voice cracking with rage and residual fear for her safety. "You almost got yourself killed."

"She was never in any danger," the sheriff assured Jed as he dismantled his weapon and returned it to the case in which he'd carried it. "From the way he was answering your questions, it was clear Henderson suspected it was a setup. He wasn't saying anything that the D.A. could use against him in court."

"But Brandon would never believe that I would let you be part of the trap to catch him." Jed clenched his hands on her shoulders. "And he was right to believe that. I never would have gone back for you if I thought you would put yourself in danger."

He had gone back for her, though. But not just her— he had waited for Rowe, who had brought in the sheriff of Blackwoods County. Together, with guidance from the Blackwoods district attorney, they had concocted their plan to bring Brandon to the justice he had eluded for far too long.

She had never been part of that plan until the sheriff and Rowe had realized Brandon was never going to implicate himself until he was certain Jed wasn't trapping him. Both men had assured her of her safety before she'd run into the garage.

And she had felt safe in the bulletproof vest she wore beneath her jacket—until Brandon had pressed the gun to her head. Then she'd felt stupid and reckless. "You're right," she agreed. "I shouldn't have gotten involved."

"Remember, it got us what we need to overturn your

murder convictions," the sheriff said as he came down from the higher level of the parking garage.

"But nothing Brandon said will get rid of the charges against me for breaking out of prison," Jed said. With a heavy sigh, he turned around—presenting the sheriff with his back, his wrists linked behind him for the cuffs.

A squeal of "Mommy" drew Erica's attention to the entrance to the parking garage. The little girl, still clad in her pajamas and bare feet, ran across the concrete.

Macy followed closely behind her. Rowe must have told her about their plan. "She got away from me. She really wanted to see you."

Erica caught the little girl up in her arms, holding her close. Her daughter had almost lost her mother. And she would lose her father. Not for life but for however long a judge sentenced him for the prison break.

"And I wanted to see you," Macy said, as she reached for her brother.

Jed hugged his sister tightly. But he stared over her head at Isobel, his eyes full of longing. He glanced back at the sheriff. "Is it okay if I spend a little time with my daughter before you take me back to Blackwoods County?"

He'd broken out of prison there, so no doubt he needed to return to the local jail in the county where he'd broken the law.

The sheriff nodded. "Your friend will be turned in to the police department here since this is where he committed his crimes."

His murders. Several innocent people had lost their lives over one man's greed and envy. Jed tensed, as if the same thought had occurred to him, but instead of blaming Brandon, he seemed to be blaming himself.

"He was never Jed's friend," Macy said.

"No," Jed agreed. "I've trusted people I shouldn't have." He glanced at Erica now.

Her stomach clenched with regret. She hadn't betrayed him as he had believed for the past three years. But her believing the worst about him was a betrayal, too. And she had done that more than once.

She wanted to apologize again, but she worried that it was too late for that. That it was already too late for them.

"I'm trusting you to come out to where the cars are parked in the alley," Sheriff York told Jed.

"I'm done running," Jed said. "I'll be out in just a few minutes."

"I'm going back to talk to my fiancé," Macy said. "I'll see if he can do something about the charges for escaping prison. Maybe he can talk to someone…" She hurried out after the sheriff.

Erica faced her sleepy-eyed daughter. "Honey, this is your father."

The little girl blinked thick lashes at her, totally confused.

"This man." She couldn't look at him when she confessed all to her daughter. "My friend Jed—he is your father. Your daddy."

Isobel turned to him for confirmation, her chocolate-brown eyes wide with shock and awe. "You're my daddy?"

Jed's throat muscles rippled as he swallowed, as if choked with emotion. "Yes, honey, I am your daddy." He held out his arms for her.

But she hung back a moment, no doubt overwhelmed with the new information. "I—I have a daddy?"

"Yes," Erica assured the little girl, sick with guilt that she had never told the child about her father.

She continued, "And he wants to spend some time with you, honey."

Before he had to go back to jail...

Erica handed Isobel over to Jed's outstretched arms and turned to leave the garage.

"Wait," he said. "Stay with us."

Either he was nervous alone with the little girl or he was concerned that the little girl would be nervous alone with him. Either reason had Erica's heart warm with love for him. Watching him with their child made her see what kind of man he really was, the man he had always been: gentle, honest and affectionate.

She had to say it—this time aloud. "I'm sorry."

"I know it wasn't your idea to interrupt my meeting with Brandon," Jed replied, absolving her of any carelessness and stupidity. "I know you thought you were perfectly safe."

She shook her head. "No. I'm sorry about..." She glanced at their daughter, who had affectionately snuggled her head into the crook of Jed's shoulder and neck. "I'm sorry that I didn't believe in you like I should have."

"Why should you have?" he asked.

Because she loved him. But she couldn't tell him that now when her mistrust had already ruined any promise they had once had for a future together.

"I should have known better," she said. And now that he and Isobel seemed so comfortable together, she had no reason to stay. She started toward the entrance to the garage.

"I never gave you the chance," he said, again absolving her.

"What?"

"To get to know me," he explained. "I never gave you the chance."

Now, for as many years as he would be locked up, she wouldn't get that chance.

HE HAD NO RIGHT TO STOP HER, so Jed just watched her walk away. Just as he hadn't when he got deployed, he didn't want her waiting for him. His returning from prison was about as likely as his return from Afghanistan had been.

"No." Erica stopped herself with the word and turned back toward him and their daughter.

"No what, Mommy?" the little girl asked, confused about what she might have done wrong.

"No. I'm not going to do this again," she said.

Macy started down the slope of the parking garage toward them. "Jed—"

"I need a minute with your brother," Erica interrupted the young woman. "Isobel, go play with your aunt for a little while. I need to talk to your daddy alone."

The little girl wriggled down from his arms and whispered, "You're in trouble now. That's Mommy's mad face."

A smile tugged at his lips…until he was alone with Erica. The little girl was right; this was her mommy's mad face. Anger tightened Erica's silky lips and hardened the pale blue of her beautiful eyes.

"What's wrong?" he asked.

"I'm not going anywhere."

"No," he agreed. "The sheriff already talked to the D.A. about making sure charges were not pressed against you for aiding and abetting me. Rowe vouched for you. You won't have to worry about yourself or Isobel."

"I'm worried about you."

"I'll be okay," he said. "No place else could ever be as bad as Blackwoods was. I'll survive my time—however long they give me." He didn't dare hope that they'd commute his sentence for the time he had already served for the crimes he hadn't committed. She walked up closer to him and lifted her hands to his shoulders, which she clasped as she pressed her body against his.

"You will survive," she said. "And I'm going to be waiting for you."

"Good," he said, breathing a sigh of relief that she wasn't going to try to deny him time with his daughter once he was done serving his time. "I want to be part of Isobel's life."

"No," she said. "*I* will be waiting for you. I'm not letting you push me away like you did before. I'm going to wait for you to be free."

Even though his heart leapt with the hope she offered him, he shook his head in rejection of her offer. "Erica, I can't ask you to do that."

"Can't or don't want to?" she asked. "Will you ever be able to forgive me for doubting you?"

"It's not so much forgiving as trusting that you won't doubt me again," he admitted.

"I should have talked to you," she said. "I should have gone to the jail where you were being held before your trial and talked to you."

"But Marcus had told you not to," he said. He completely accepted that his lawyer had manipulated her.

"I shouldn't have trusted him over you."

"I trusted him, too," he said with a weary sigh. He hadn't thought Marcus was smart enough to lie, but then he had had Brandon, the master manipulator, coaching him. "We both made mistakes."

"Then don't make another one," she warned him. "Don't push me away if you really want me."

He couldn't have her putting her life on hold any more now than he had been able to years ago. She was a mother; she and her daughter needed more than he could offer them. So he gripped her shoulders and gently pushed her back. "Go..."

She blinked, as if fighting back tears. "I hope you're pushing me away because you can't forgive me and not because you think you're doing what's best for me. Thinking that you hate me or that you don't want me—" her voice cracked with emotion "—that isn't what's best for me. That hurts me."

And hurting her hurt him; pain clutched his heart. He loved her. He had always loved her. That was why he wanted more for her than him.

"I can't..." he murmured, unable to say more.

"Can't forgive me?" She nodded in response to her own question before he could even form a reply. "I don't blame you. I can't forgive myself."

As she turned for the entrance again, where his sister and daughter waited just beyond hearing, he reached out. Grabbing her arm, he whirled her back to him and pulled her into his arms. "I can't let you go again."

Her breath escaped in a shaky gasp of surprise. "Jed..."

"I love you, Erica," he said, finally declaring the feelings he had denied for far too long, "so I should be unselfish. I shouldn't ask you to wait for me, but..."

"I would anyway," she said. "I waited when you went to Afghanistan, and without even knowing it, I waited while you were in prison. There has never been anyone else for me but you."

He lowered his mouth and took hers in a deep, possessive kiss. Her lips parted as if she breathed him in, as if she needed him for air. As if she needed him as he needed her.

"I love you, Jed," she said. "And that's why I never should have doubted you."

"Maybe that's why you did," he said. "Because your love made you vulnerable and scared." He held her closely. "You never need to be again. I will come home to you and Isobel. I will come back."

"You never have to go away," Macy said, her face flushing with embarrassment at getting caught eavesdropping.

Jed flashed back to all the times, while they were growing up, that his pesky little sister had barged in on him with a girlfriend. She had jealously wanted all his attention back then because their parents had given her none of theirs. But she seemed very willing to share him with Erica. As smart as she was, she would have realized before he had how much he loved and needed to be with Erica.

"The district attorney, Drake Ketchum, waived all the charges against you," Macy said, her voice shaking with excitement.

"Why?" Jed asked, too cynical now to believe it was possible.

"You served three years for crimes you hadn't committed," Erica said. "You shouldn't have to serve any more time."

Jed stared at his sister. "Did Rowe have something to do with this?"

"No," she said. "The D.A. is using you as his star witness against the warden."

Jed chuckled. He'd been right to be cynical. Nobody was selfless except for the woman in his arms, who had willingly put her life at risk for his. "I take it that he doesn't want me showing up in court to testify in an orange jumpsuit."

"Who cares what his motive is?" Erica asked. "You're a free man, Jedidiah Kleyn."

"I don't want to be a free man," he said with sudden realization.

"But, Jed," she said, her eyes wide with shock, "you served three years already—"

"No." He dropped to one knee on the cold concrete. "I don't want to be a free man. I want to be your man, Erica. I don't just want to be Isobel's father. I want to be your husband…if you'll have me. If you can trust me…"

For the first time since he had pulled her into the nightmare that had been his life, she cried, tears streaming down her face. "I trust you, Jed. I trust that you'll be a gentle, loving father and a loyal, protective husband." She wrapped her arms around his shoulders and hugged him tightly. "I will marry you."

Her acceptance meant more to him than finally clearing his name. That had been all about his past. She and their daughter were his future. "Now I'm the luckiest man in the world."

Finally the promise of their first meeting and that instant connection was fulfilled. That promise had been tested and strained and had nearly broken over the past three years. But now it was a promise that they would keep for the rest of their lives.

Epilogue

"You better get used to that side of the bars," Drake Ketchum taunted him. "You're never getting out now."

Jefferson had already heard the news. The district attorney definitely had a star witness in Jedidiah Kleyn. No one would doubt his testimony now.

"And you're not getting to Kleyn before the trial. There's no bounty—no amount of reward you can offer for someone to risk hurting him. He's well protected."

And damn near impossible to kill, Jefferson had already discovered. But with all his time alone behind these damn bars, he had figured out who wasn't protected—who was so damn cocky that he thought he couldn't lose.

But it wasn't just the trial Ketchum was going to lose. It was his life.

* * * * *

SUSPENSE

COMING NEXT MONTH
AVAILABLE MAY 8, 2012

#1347 COLBY LAW
Colby, TX
Debra Webb

#1348 SECRET AGENDA
Cooper Security
Paula Graves

#1349 OBSESSION
Guardians of Coral Cove
Carol Ericson

#1350 THE MARINE NEXT DOOR
The Precinct: Task Force
Julie Miller

#1351 PRIVATE SECURITY
The Delancey Dynasty
Mallory Kane

#1352 WHEN SHE WASN'T LOOKING
HelenKay Dimon

You can find more information on upcoming Harlequin®
titles, free excerpts and more at www.Harlequin.com.

HICNM0412

REQUEST YOUR FREE BOOKS!
2 FREE NOVELS PLUS 2 FREE GIFTS!

 Harlequin®

INTRIGUE®

BREATHTAKING ROMANTIC SUSPENSE

YES! Please send me 2 FREE Harlequin Intrigue® novels and my 2 FREE gifts (gifts are worth about $10). After receiving them, if I don't wish to receive any more books, I can return the shipping statement marked "cancel." If I don't cancel, I will receive 6 brand-new novels every month and be billed just $4.49 per book in the U.S. or $5.24 per book in Canada. That's a saving of at least 14% off the cover price! It's quite a bargain! Shipping and handling is just 50¢ per book in the U.S. and 75¢ per book in Canada.* I understand that accepting the 2 free books and gifts places me under no obligation to buy anything. I can always return a shipment and cancel at any time. Even if I never buy another book, the two free books and gifts are mine to keep forever.

182/382 HDN FEQ2

Name	(PLEASE PRINT)	
Address		Apt. #
City	State/Prov.	Zip/Postal Code

Signature (if under 18, a parent or guardian must sign)

Mail to the **Reader Service:**
IN U.S.A.: P.O. Box 1867, Buffalo, NY 14240-1867
IN CANADA: P.O. Box 609, Fort Erie, Ontario L2A 5X3

Not valid for current subscribers to Harlequin Intrigue books.

**Are you a subscriber to Harlequin Intrigue books
and want to receive the larger-print edition?
Call 1-800-873-8635 or visit www.ReaderService.com.**

* Terms and prices subject to change without notice. Prices do not include applicable taxes. Sales tax applicable in N.Y. Canadian residents will be charged applicable taxes. Offer not valid in Quebec. This offer is limited to one order per household. All orders subject to credit approval. Credit or debit balances in a customer's account(s) may be offset by any other outstanding balance owed by or to the customer. Please allow 4 to 6 weeks for delivery. Offer available while quantities last.

Your Privacy—The Reader Service is committed to protecting your privacy. Our Privacy Policy is available online at www.ReaderService.com or upon request from the Reader Service.

We make a portion of our mailing list available to reputable third parties that offer products we believe may interest you. If you prefer that we not exchange your name with third parties, or if you wish to clarify or modify your communication preferences, please visit us at www.ReaderService.com/consumerschoice or write to us at Reader Service Preference Service, P.O. Box 9062, Buffalo, NY 14269. Include your complete name and address.

HIIIB

INTRIGUE

DANGER LURKS AROUND EVERY CORNER
WITH AUTHOR

PAULA GRAVES

CATCH A NEW INSTALLMENT OF

Four years ago, Megan Cooper Randall buried her husband,
thinking he died a hero while battling rebels. The last thing she
expects is former Pentagon lawyer Evan Pike to show up and
state her deceased husband was a carefully targeted victim.
With mercenaries hot on their heels, Evan and Megan
have to work fast to uncover past conspiracies and fight
for the chance to build a future together.

SECRET AGENDA

The truth will be revealed
May 2012

May is Mystery Month!

With six titles to choose from every month, uncover
your love for breathtaking romantic suspense
with Harlequin® Intrigue today!

www.Harlequin.com

HI69615

*Colby Investigator Lyle McCaleb is on the case.
But can he protect Sadie Gilmore from her haunting past?*

*Harlequin Intrigue® presents a new installment
in Debra Webb's miniseries, COLBY, TX.*

Enjoy a sneak peek of COLBY LAW.

With the shotgun hanging at her side, she made it as far as the porch steps, when the driver's side door opened. Sadie knew the deputies in Coryell County. Her visitor wasn't any of them. A boot hit the ground, stirring the dust. Something deep inside her braced for a new kind of trouble. As the driver emerged, Sadie's gaze moved upward, over the gleaming black door and the tinted window to a black Stetson and dark sunglasses. She couldn't quite make out the details of the man's face but some extra sense that had nothing to do with what she could see set her on edge.

Another boot hit the ground and the door closed. Her visual inspection swept over long legs cinched in comfortably worn denim, a lean waist and broad shoulders testing the seams of a shirt that hadn't come off the rack at any store where she shopped, finally zeroing in on the man's face just as he removed the dark glasses.

The weapon almost slipped from her grasp. Her heart bucked hard twice, then skidded to a near halt.

Lyle McCaleb.

"What the...devil?" whispered past her lips.

Unable to move a muscle, she watched in morbid fascination as he hooked the sunglasses on to his hip pocket and strode toward the house—toward her. Sadie wouldn't have been able to summon a warning that he was trespassing had her life depended on it.

Lyle glanced at the shotgun as he reached up and removed his hat. "Expecting company?"

As if her heart had suddenly started to pump once more, kicking her brain into gear, fury blasted through her frozen muscles. "What do you want, Lyle McCaleb?"

"Seeing as you didn't know I was coming, that couldn't be for me." He gave a nod toward her shotgun.

This could not be happening. Seven years he'd been gone. This was…this was… "I have nothing to say to you." She turned her back to him and walked away. Who did he think he was, showing up here like this after all this time? It was crazy. He was crazy!

"I know I'm the last person on this earth you want to see."

Her feet stopped when she wanted to keep going. To get inside the house and slam the door and dead bolt it.

"We need to talk."

The stakes are high as Lyle fights for the woman he loves. But can he solve the case in time to save an innocent life?

Find out in COLBY LAW
Available May 2012 from Harlequin Intrigue®
wherever books are sold.

Copyright © 2012 Debra Webb

HIEXP0512